The COOKIE CRUMBLES

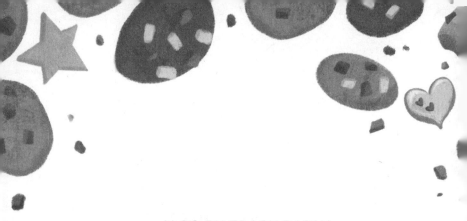

ALSO BY TRACY BADUA

Freddie vs. the Family Curse
The Takeout

ALSO BY ALECHIA DOW

Just a Pinch of Magic

The COOKIE CRUMBLES

TRACY BADUA & ALECHIA DOW

Quill Tree Books
An Imprint of HarperCollinsPublishers

Quill Tree Books is an imprint of HarperCollins Publishers.

Library of Congress Control Number: 2023944473
ISBN 978-0-06-325458-9

Typography by Andrea Vandergrift
24 25 26 27 28 LBC 5 4 3 2 1
First Edition

*To the bakers who never met a pastry
they didn't want to bake, and to
the busters who never met a mystery
they didn't want to solve.
This book is for you.*

—T. B. and A. D.

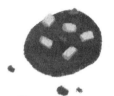

DAY ONE

THE PAST IN PASTRY

LAILA'S JOURNAL ENTRY

Generally speaking, cookies don't kill people.

Cookies save people. Cookies are the reason some people get out of bed in the morning. You've got chocolate cookies, vanilla cookies, breakfast cookies, macarons, alfajores, whoopie pies, and all kinds in between. I mean, you can basically have an entire conversation with someone just by exchanging cookies.

Side note: I wish I could eat a cookie right now. My nerves need one.

Anyway, as you can tell, and as Stevie Wonder once said—which I'm paraphrasing—I was made to love cookies. I was made to make them. Sell them. Become a cookie tycoon, CEO of Cookie Corp. My future will be full of cookies.

So it was a terrible surprise when some people

claimed that one of my cookies nearly killed someone. Like, *huge* surprise.

I know it wasn't my fault (not everyone is convinced), but my best friend, Lucy—journalist extraordinaire in training—wants to write a story about the competition anyway. When she shoved a pen at me earlier and said that writing this all down would give us a timeline for the entire first day, I said yes, though it made me nervous. Lucy may think that we have to solve this before someone tries to dish out another service of death or . . . I get arrested, but if there's one thing I know, it's best to let sleeping dogs lie. Or is it lay? Doesn't matter, you know what I mean.

Lucy's pretty smart. So she knows how bad this could be for me if they investigate. I trust she's doing all this for the right reasons, which is why I'm here bent over a notebook, detailing our first and worst day at the Golden Cookie Competition.

Gulp, my mouth's as dry as a low-fat shortbread. Right. Let's go all the way back to before we arrived at Sunderland Academy. That's the best place to start. No attempted murder (yet), only excitement.

And this time I'll try not to mention cookies so much.

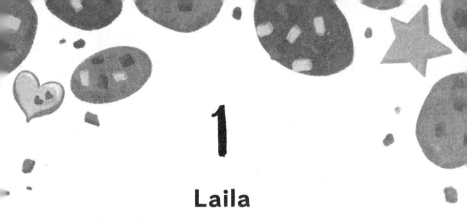

1

Laila

IT WAS EARLY on a summery Friday morning, and I was at home, draped over my bed, thinking about life and the upcoming competition that weekend. I'd already entered and placed first in the qualification round for our town; now I just needed to compete for the chance of a lifetime. The chance to do great, big things.

The chance to win not only the coveted Golden Cookie award but a free ride to Sunderland Academy next year. One of the best, and therefore most expensive, boarding high schools in the country that, bonus, had one of the best precollege journalism programs. Lucy had already gotten accepted a few months ago, though her parents hadn't quite figured out how to afford it yet—which was why she was coming along to the competition.

More on that later.

Anyway, Lucy and I wouldn't be going to high school for another year. Thanks to weirdly drawn school district lines, this would be our last year at the same school—possibly in the same town too—if we didn't figure out how to go to Sunderland together. And that'd be a disaster.

If I got into Sunderland, we'd share a dorm, catch the bus home on the weekends, and continue along with the greatness that is our friendship.

We *needed* to go to school together. Outside of Mom, Lucy was all I had.

Lucy lived on the other side of town. She had a nice house and a nice dog—unlike my cat, Catsby, who bit me every time I came too close to her fluffy tummy. Lucy had it all. Good grades, oodles of friends, shiny black hair that still looked beautiful after a sudden, terrible gust of wind, and a wardrobe of well-fitting clothes. But she wanted more, and she was far too ambitious for her own good.

She wanted to be the next Barbara Walters or, better yet, Ariella Wilborn. I'd never heard anyone talk about a journalist the way Lucy talked about Ariella Wilborn, like she's Captain Marvel.

While Lucy had ambition, talent, and smarts, I had cookies. Everybody's got their thing, the special talent they'll use for the rest of their lives, right? Well, food? That was my thing.

Not only cookies. In my spare time on the weekends, I'd (illegally) staged at restaurants around town. I'd learned how to make a mean spicy salmon roll with red pepper aioli, fry chicken according to an old Black woman's great-grandmother's recipe (the trick was marinating it in milk), and construct a mouthwatering burger using the right ratios of different types of ground beef. I'd assisted in dinner rushes, meal prep, and once, when Mom was working, I snuck out at five a.m. to help the local baker with his daily bread bake. Food was so totally my thing.

And that was another reason I had to go to Sunderland: its superstar culinary program would boost my special talents so I'd get to bake, expertly and happily, for the rest of my life.

"Laila, you packed? You need anything?" Mom walked into my room, the braids on her hair disheveled and flapping all over the place. She was in her nursing scrubs, and there were dark circles under her eyes, though she hadn't yet left for work at the hospital on the other side of our small suburb, Fable Creek.

I had just been thinking I could've used a new pair of shoes to replace my tight-around-the-toes ones, but they weren't a priority. "Nope, got everything I need."

She'd been single momming me since Dad passed away from cancer when I was seven. We lost our house because of the medical and funeral bills, and then we got evicted from our last apartment. Mom was a guilty wreck about it. She thought it was all her fault everything fell apart. It was my job to let her know it wasn't, that we could still achieve big things even if we had to start from a lower ledge than everyone else. Me winning the Golden Cookie would be good for her too.

And until then, I could stretch my time with these small shoes a little longer.

"How are you feeling about the competition?" She sat down on the edge of my bed and brushed a few frizzy curls behind my ear. I looked up into her hazel eyes. My eyes were all Dad's: dark brown to match our dark brown skin and dark brown hair; I was a walking chocolate bar. While Mom was lithe and fragile, I was thick. Kids at school used to say it's because I ate all the time (I didn't), but now I knew that was how my body was, and Mom's was different. Despite those differences, I still looked like her. The same nose, same knobby chin, same Cupid's bow lips.

"I'm fine," I answered, closing my eyes as she patted my head. "Maybe a bit nervous."

"You were nervous when you had to qualify, remember?" She nudged my shoulder. "And you came in first place. You didn't break a sweat."

I looked at her and smiled as a knot formed in the pit of

my stomach. "Yeah, but all the kids going to the competition are winners too." What I didn't mention was that all of them were rich and talented and came from upper-crust families. They had all the advantages. Unlike us. "They're the best of the best."

"Hmm," she hummed. "So are you."

That seemed to untwist the knot a little bit. Maybe she was right about all that other stuff not mattering in the kitchen. It wasn't about where we've been, but where we're going. "I can do this. And besides, Lucy'll be there."

"You two . . ." Mom shook her head. "You can't be apart, huh?"

"She's my person," I retorted. "She gets me." And I got her too. The thought of not going to school with her made me feel like I was stuck in a black hole of sadness. The same way I felt for a few months after Dad died. Like my world was getting smaller and smaller and I'd be left all alone, floating in space.

Mom, using the last few moments she had before starting a long shift, helped me finish packing my bag. She carefully folded my purple apron, which Dad bought me when I started to cook and Lucy helped remake into a larger one. That way Dad would always be with me, cheering me on.

"You're brave and talented, Laila, and there's nowhere you can't go. Nothing you can't do," he used to say. Whenever

I was feeling lonely and lost, I tried to remember that. Repeat it aloud until I felt it.

"When's the van coming?" Mom asked when my clothes were neatly folded. She rose and put her hands on her back, stretching.

I sat on my suitcase to try to get it flat. Sure, we'd be gone only three days, but I needed my supplies. Specific extracts I'd made myself, like my lemon oil with lemon verbena leaves and my peachy vanilla. The competition rules said we couldn't bring in our own materials, but I got special permission for these because Sunderland's kitchen didn't carry them. "In ten minutes."

"Good luck, honey." She put a hand on my shoulder as I stood up. "I believe in you. And remember, I'll be at work tonight, and then the Emergency Nurses of America conference this weekend. So only call if you need to, okay? Lucy's parents said they'd be watching the live stream and sitting by the phone if you girls want anything."

I agreed and swept her up in the most rib-shattering hug I could manage. She gasped only once. "Love you, Mom. I got this, promise." I meant it. This was the opportunity of a lifetime, and there was no way I'd let it pass me by.

She kissed my cheek and took off as the sun began to peek through the fog. And I thought, as I brought my suitcase onto the porch, watching her leave, *Wow, it's chilly for a summer morning. Unusual.* But had I known the weekend that was about to happen, I would have realized that unusual was definitely better than attempted murder.

Most things are better than murder.

A van pulled up outside my house at exactly half-past seven. It was a white van, the kind that schools use for teachers' night out. I knew because one night while I was helping at our local gastropub, I caught the teachers having a dinner meeting and getting a little too liberal with the cocktails. They piled in the van after. Most likely this van. Remembering how queasy they looked, I was apprehensive about sliding inside now.

Until Lucy came out and scrutinized my suitcase. She scrunched her flat, light brown nose. "It's only three days."

I shoved my suitcase in the back and jumped into the van. "You'll thank me if you need to look up a baking term in one of my cookbooks." Meanwhile, I eyed her backpack as I buckled myself in. "Let me guess, you brought empty notebooks, a voice recorder, one hoodie, one pair of jeans, and a few books about the science of journalism."

She gave me a sheepish grin that all but confirmed it. "The necessities."

We settled into our seats in a row in front of two other contestants, from two different middle schools. Lucy had made a dossier on each of these other soon-to-be eighth graders and had me study them for their weaknesses. She was always prepared like that.

I peered behind us. The blond girl with gold, cupcake-shaped earrings was Philippa Willingsworth—a future debutante, because those existed and people were them. She was so well-off she went to a private academy two towns over, where only the rich lived. They had a multilevel Starbucks and overpriced mall stores hanging out on their main street. Worst of all, she was good. Supergood. The kind of good where she'd most likely have her own restaurant one day. So good she didn't need the scholarship. She didn't need to compete.

Her weakness: couldn't make a Bavarian mousse to save her life.

And then there was Micah Dae, cradling some weird plant on his lap. He was from the sister burb of Fable Creek called Fable Falls, where middle-class families were living their best lives. His parents owned a casual-dining restaurant, where he worked the cash register three nights a week in between Junior Botany Society meetings. Despite being a nerd, or maybe *because* he was a nerd, he was totally cute.

His weakness: a bit too classic (aka boring) with his flavor choices.

All in all, with the other two contestants arriving at Sunderland in a different van, I liked my odds. Which was probably what both Micah and Philippa were thinking as they sized me up.

Micah glanced at me and my brain blanked. "I brought some cookies for everyone. As a way to . . . like . . . say hi." He shifted the plant off his lap and dug out a small plastic bag of mangled, crumbly dark brown cookies from his hoodie pocket.

They didn't *look* enticing, but I accepted one to be polite. So did Lucy and Philippa.

Once I took a bite of the soft, light cookie, I realized my initial assessment was wrong. Very wrong. They were ginger-molasses cookies, which sounded standard, but they contained a whole lot of delicious spices I was sure Micah thought was his secret blend.

Micah and the other contestants didn't know my strengths and weaknesses because they didn't have a dossier made by their best friend about me. But if they did, they'd know that I had a baking superpower: I could take a bite of something and be able to tell exactly what was in it. I never missed an ingredient. Which was why I was able to quickly figure out that these cookies had the traditional seasonings of allspice, nutmeg, ginger, and cardamom, but also some Chinese five-spice powder: a blend of ground cloves, special peppercorns, fennel, star anise, and a cinnamon stick. It was a perfectly warm explosion of flavor.

We all demolished our cookies in seconds. Philippa tossed him a glance and then stared out the window without another word. Probably grasping that Micah was real competition. Lucy, on the other hand, looked somewhat relieved. The ginger might've temporarily helped calm her upset stomach. While my own stomach soured as I began recalibrating.

In Micah's dossier, it said his weakness was that he was too classic with his flavor choices. If these cookies were any indication, the dossier didn't consider how badly he and the other contestants wanted to win or that a weakness at his level still produced seriously good cookies. Now I had to think about my own weaknesses and wonder if they affected my baking as much as his seemed not to.

Mine: tended to panic under pressure and would literally do anything for Mom and Lucy. And little did the other contestants know that one of them was sitting beside me, still the teensiest bit green, clutching a book about cookies.

Lucy's: had no idea about cooking, baking, cookies, or the food community, but desperately wanted to get a broad range of writing samples together for Sunderland's Ariella Wilborn Journalism Scholarship by next week. She already had half a dozen pieces from her time on the school paper. I thought they were all great, yet the coach that the scholarship committee provided to help guide students with their applications had said Lucy's pieces might all be too similar or simple for the scholarship. Based on the coach's assessment, this was Lucy's last, best chance to write some new pieces showcasing a wide variety of her skills: something scholarship-worthy. She was in it to win it this weekend as much as I was.

"Thanks for the cookie. It was delicious." I put the cheeriest tone in my voice as I spoke to Micah. He nodded before settling into his seat and putting his plant on his lap. I tried to keep cool as I turned my back on my rivals. "How long does it take to get there?"

Lucy glanced down at her phone. "It's normally an hour, but with all the construction on the highway, my map app says we'll be there in two hours."

"Ugh, two hours in a *van*?" Philippa sighed loudly. "I could've had my driver take me, but I was trying to escape my family. I didn't need their . . . pressure, you know?" She smiled, and I felt it was suspicious, because why, if she had her own ride, would she opt for the van? It was likely because she wanted to suss us all out, get a feel for the competition. When we didn't return her smile, she sniffed. "Anyway, I didn't think it was going to take this long. Probably should've gone with the driver—would've taken the same time, but at least it would have been more comfortable."

Micah only cocked an eyebrow at no one in particular, yanked his hood down over his short black hair, and turned on his side away from us. I guess he was done saying hello.

And I thought, *Wow. He's so cute.* But also, *Why isn't he more excited?* This was the competition of a lifetime. You'd think he'd take this chance to figure us all out so he could beat us later. Instead, he seemed bored. Weird, right?

Although maybe he was just tired. Or maybe he was shy and giving the cookies was the most he could do? I didn't know. Didn't really matter, because I was focused on winning. No matter what.

LUCY'S JOURNAL ENTRY

Thunder cracks overhead. We received reports that the streets are flooded. The cellular service bars flit from one to nothing on my phone. Laila, the other competitors, and I have all been stuck in our rooms since the police and the EMTs left. The authorities spent some time interviewing everyone and documenting evidence while the EMTs checked vitals and scribbled on charts, but then the lights flickered from the growing storm. They quickly took the victim away on a stretcher and fled before the rain got worse, but not before promising to send more investigators.

But I know how to read between the lines, or, in this case, the way the authorities wouldn't make eye contact with any of us and the way they hunched together and whispered their hypotheses to each other. I knew they were hiding something, so I snuck closer, pretending to retrieve my pen from the worktable (in reality, I brought a thousand pens with me). That's when I caught the unmistakable, chill-inducing mention of "foul play." Someone set out to cause harm, and it's still unknown who that someone is.

We've been asked to stay in our rooms as a safety measure, in case the power goes out. But with a suspicious accident and worsening weather, we don't know if the competition is still happening tomorrow.

With nowhere to go, Laila and I have only one thing to do: write down everything. Laila doesn't seem to be as enthusiastic as I am about digging into the details of this near tragedy. But it's the only way we'll get to the bottom of this and, maybe, the only way we can keep ourselves safe.

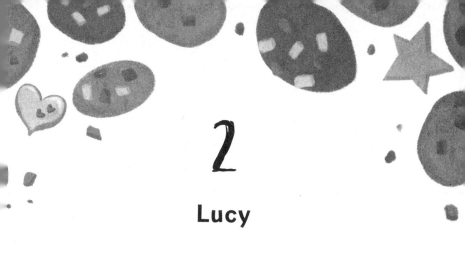

2

Lucy

THE BUMPY ROADS up to Sunderland Academy set off an epic bout of car sickness. Laila waving the dossiers in my face and trying to get me to read a whole tiny-print book on cookies made it much, much worse. Micah's ginger cookie, though delicious, helped for only a few precious minutes.

I unlatched the window, pushed it open to its maximum two inches, and tried to inhale as much fresh air as possible.

"Better?" Laila asked.

"Blargh" is all I managed to respond. The air outside was heavy, not as refreshing as it could have been. I blamed the humidity on the dark clouds overhead: good thing this competition was indoors. Conveniently all in one building, in fact. We wouldn't have to leave for anything.

The van bucked as we sped down empty roads and rolled

over the narrow stone bridge to the Sunderland campus. The main road was under construction, the school administrators and city officials taking advantage of summer break to complete its major roadwork. The campus would be all ours for the Golden Cookie Competition.

Normally, the campus would be limited to only the competitors, two judges, and a competition coordinator, but I asked to go on behalf of our school paper. For the Ariella Wilborn Journalism Scholarship I desperately needed to attend Sunderland, I had to show off some of my other writing skills, not just the ones used to write about the sixth-grade candy fundraiser or the caption for the picture of the new snake in Mr. Reyes's classroom. This high-stakes cookie competition would be one great way to flex my sensory-detail muscles. Plus, it'd give me an opportunity to firm up the surprise profile I was doing on Laila, not just for the scholarship writing sample but for submission to our town paper as well: Laila deserved all the good coverage for how hard she's been working on her baking. She deserved all the good everything after how tough a time she and her mom have had the past few years.

When our newspaper staff adviser and I spoke to the Sunderland administrators, they were more than happy to have me come too, especially after I mentioned it'd be a sneak peek of what my high school years there would look like.

And lucky for me, Laila was assigned a double room with two twin beds, so it'd be like one big sleepover. Well, one big sleepover that my whole future at Sunderland with my best friend was riding on.

So there I was, scrunched in the back seat, trying not to vomit, attempting to brainstorm any other ideas for impressing the Sunderland scholarship committee. The image of Tonya, the scholarship coach, flipping through my portfolio was burned into my brain. She'd graduated from Sunderland a decade ago and was excited to "give back" by helping future students. But that excitement faded along with her smile as she turned the pages of my application package. Then she had gently asked whether my printer had malfunctioned and failed to print the rest of my work.

No, the truth was that my existing portfolio felt as flimsy and fleeting as cotton candy, but that wasn't my fault. It was Peter's, our jerk of an editor in chief for the school paper. He shut me out as coeditor yet somehow still held a grudge against me for rejecting his invitation to the school dance. He made sure I covered only the dullest of newspaper-related tasks. Nagging the school clubs for their event schedules and rewriting the maintenance staff's updates on the resodding of the field? That was all me. I never got the cheating scandals, the protests against the school dress code, the allegations of discrimination in the academic heptathlon team.

Luckily, someone in the Sunderland admissions committee saw the potential in me and my stellar grades: I pinched myself twice when I learned I got into their journalism program, home of my no-nonsense, respected-everywhere newscaster idol, Ariella Wilborn. But the price tag of this place was too high. My parents had already told me my options were this scholarship or them putting their money into moving us to a better school district across the state as soon as the end of summer.

For any hope of following my dreams at Sunderland and staying best friends with Laila, I needed to prove to the scholarship committee that I could live up to the admissions folks' faith in me. According to Tonya, that meant demonstrating I was a serious journalist who could cover a whole range of topics well, not just prettily arrange a schedule of the volleyball team's next home games.

Next to me, Laila gasped. "There it is!"

The tree-lined road spilled the van out onto the sprawling Sunderland campus, all white pillars and stately red brick. Even Micah, who I swear had been fast asleep for the last two hours, yanked his hood off to peer out of the window as we pulled into the cul-de-sac for the residence halls. Wide, empty walkways crisscrossed the expanse of neatly trimmed grass around us. The only person in sight was a man in his thirties, in a gold-and-black-striped collared shirt and dark slacks despite the heat, waving at us.

The van slowed to a stop, and I couldn't have stumbled out of that back seat fast enough. My foot caught on a seat belt, and the only thing keeping me from splatting onto the asphalt was the man's quick grasp of my forearm.

"Are you all right?" he asked. "You look ill." His pale white skin was flushed red from the heat, as if he realized too late that dark fabric was not the best choice for this summer weather. His short, wavy black hair clung to his temples with sweat, and his round-rimmed glasses were slightly fogged up.

"If Lucy's sick, maybe she shouldn't be here," Philippa said, taking a step back from me. "We can't have her spreading whatever it is. I'd hate for anything to happen to the judges."

I glared at her before throwing a thankful smile at my hero of the minute. "I'm fine. And I'm just here to observe, not bake. Don't mind me."

"She gets carsick," Laila said, coming to my aid like she always did.

Laila handed me my duffel bag as our driver, Coach Clark, the wrestling coach and culinary arts instructor, closed the back of the van.

"I'll see you kids on Sunday afternoon," he said, already punching the address of our school into his phone.

"Wait, you're not staying?" Laila asked.

Coach Clark slid into the driver's seat and buckled himself in. "Nope. School's only paying me to drive here and back, then doing it again after the competition. I'd love to stay and chat, but those rain clouds . . ."

He didn't finish his sentence. The van lurched forward and he sped back through the school's iron gates, the only car on the road as far as the eye could see.

The man who caught me stepped back and swept his arms out like he was performing a magic trick. "Welcome, all, to Sunderland Academy, home of the Golden Cookie Competition." He paused for applause, and Laila was the only one who obliged. "I'm Noah St. John, assistant to Chef Remi Boucre, one of our esteemed judges. I'm also coordinator of this year's competition, so I'll fill you in on our schedule. First we'll deposit your belongings in your rooms, then it's off to the kitchen for your first round."

Micah blinked. "Wow, we're really diving right in, then."

Noah smiled wide. "Of course we are! We only have three days and six challenges to assess which of you five competitors deserves a full-ride admission to this acclaimed institution." Everyone shifted on their feet at the intensity of the schedule, and Noah cocked an eyebrow. "That's right, six challenges to test your skills. In the mornings you'll perform a technical feat of the judges' choosing, and in the afternoons you'll make a showstopping masterpiece that'll demonstrate your talent and artistry. Now, if you please, follow me."

Then he spun and marched toward the residence hall. He held the door open for us, Philippa taking selfies, Micah describing our surroundings to his potted plant, and Laila with her jaw open, like she was trying to inhale every detail of the place. Laila and I left our bags in our assigned dorm room. Two boring, matching desks and beds hugged the plain white walls, and a wide window overlooked a shut-off fountain in the courtyard. All the competitors were clustered together on the same floor of this vacant residence hall. It was unnerving, our small group alone in this massive building, but the noise of everyone else knocking their luggage around helped disguise the emptiness.

Noah was rushing us to the kitchen, so I had only a minute to dig out my notebook. I also grabbed the digital SLR camera that the school newspaper adviser made my parents and me sign a dozen liability forms for before checking it out. It took a few more seconds to find an extra pen under all those packets of SkyFlakes crackers my well-meaning grandma had apparently snuck into my luggage. Laila spent that minute fishing her purple polka-dot apron out of her unnecessarily large suitcase.

Then Noah led the way to a set of double doors, which

he pulled open to reveal a bright, airy space dotted with six spotless workstations. Each featured its own huge, gleaming mixer, and below the workstations sat big plastic flour and sugar bins and half racks for the competitors' creations. Laila murmured something about Hobart, but my eyes instead went to the two other competitors already there.

The girl, short with wavy black hair and teal-rimmed glasses, jumped to her feet when we entered, like we'd startled her. "Hi, I'm Maeve Issawi," she said quietly.

The other competitor took a moment to drag his cold, green eyes away from his phone to greet us. "Jaden."

Laila stiffened when Jaden's gaze landed on her.

"You again," he muttered.

His words struck me as odd. There was definitely a story between them that I didn't know about yet, and it seemed to have not been a happy ending. I'd have to ask Laila later. I wondered why she hadn't said anything to me about it before.

We all introduced ourselves, and Jaden raised a perfectly arched, dark brown eyebrow when it was my turn.

"She's not a competitor?" he asked. "Then what's she doing here?"

"I'm writing a piece on the competition for our school paper."

Jaden crossed his arms. "No one else came with a press

crew. She shouldn't be allowed to stay." He swiveled his gaze to Laila. "You trying to cheat again or something? Is that what she's here for?"

Laila gasped before her face set in a narrow-eyed, clenched-jawed, you'd-better-get-out-of-the-way grimace. "Ha. You wish I needed to cheat to beat you because you're a poor loser." She let a long breath loose. "Everyone here got in because of pure talent."

Laila was right. The dossiers I'd compiled on all the competitors proved that this group was the best of the best. Just-turned-thirteen Maeve Issawi may have stood three inches shorter than the rest of us, but my research showed she was a whiz in a chemistry lab and a giant in the kitchen. She was from the same town as Philippa, but with Maeve's quirky, secondhand-store style, you wouldn't guess her family to be the luxury-living, ramen-fusion mogul Issawis known all over the world.

Her weakness: one small mishap could throw off her concentration entirely, which could be lethal in a timed competition like Golden Cookie.

Not to say that Jaden Parker wasn't a serious competitor, though. He tagged along on his indie-filmmaker parents' treks across the world, honing his baking skills and picking up techniques along the way. He'd won several competitions before too, though not against Laila, it seemed.

His weakness: he was a little too lofty with his flavor combinations.

"Now, now, no need for that kind of conflict here." Noah stepped in, his voice kind. He had his hands splayed out, like he was trying to calm some wild tigers instead of a group of middle schoolers. "This is a friendly competition. Yes, one of you will be named the winner each day, with an overall winner named on Sunday, but it's our hope that you all win by forming lasting bonds from our weekend here together."

Laila and I smiled at each other, but over her shoulder, I caught Jaden rolling his eyes. None of us were here to make friends, and I couldn't wait to see Laila wipe the floor with the likes of this Jaden guy. Then Laila's gaze slipped away from me, and I almost laughed to see where it landed: on Micah, who was rolling up his sleeves to reveal the muscles in his forearms.

Noah, satisfied that the competitors weren't going to tear each other apart, lowered his hands. "Miss Lucy is staying. The Sunderland administration approved this exception weeks ago. As for the rest of you, go ahead and find your stations. The judges will be here shortly."

I spotted Laila's name in fancy black cursive on a white card, perched atop one of the long wooden benches, and Laila practically skipped over to it. While she skimmed her fingertips across her workspace, I glanced around for an out-of-the-way place to post up and observe.

"Over here, Miss Lucy." Noah beckoned to me from a station at the front of the room. "This is closer to where the judges will be. You can pull up a seat behind them and get a good view of the action. Just try not to distract the competitors while they're working or block the live stream cameras. The connection on those is already spotty as it is."

I smiled, thankful for the inclusion. That brush with Jaden made me wonder if I was wasting my time even trying to make my portfolio shine with some new pieces—was I good enough to turn this weekend's events into a reason for Sunderland to field my tuition for four years?—and I appreciated Noah's kindness.

I grabbed a three-legged stool nearby, and he was right: I did get a good view. I could see each of the competitors checking out their new homes for the next few days. In fact, everyone could see what everyone else was doing: not a moment of privacy, unless they walked into one of those fancy refrigerator closets at the back of the room. On the far wall was a digital clock that would count down, in red foot-high numbers, the time left in the round.

The competition materials had proclaimed that this event would be live streamed for the first time this year, as a small consolation for the foundation requesting parents not attend.

Apparently, in years prior, overzealous parents had yelled at their competitor kids in front of everyone and argued with the judges. Having a parent-free weekend did make this feel a little more summer-campy, but in a good way. Laila and I were going to get a real peek into what our unsupervised dorm-roomie life would be like in a couple of years.

I balanced my notebook on my leg and began taking notes, while Noah went over the rules of the kitchen and the competition for everyone. He pointed to a thick white binder he'd placed on each workstation, complete with the many, many pages of Golden Cookie Competition rules, as well as Sunderland Academy policies for our summer stay. Sunderland had so many restrictions and requirements for not only the competitors but the people it appointed to carry out its famed competition. Maintaining its prestige through top talent, elite judges, and zero scandal was all in Sunderland's plan to attract wealthy donors. From the looks of this high-tech kitchen, that plan was working.

Three days, six rounds at either two or three hours each. Competitors would be judged on their skills: following directions, improvising flavors, adapting under pressure, and highlighting their kitchen prowess.

And, as if on cue, in strode the two judges. I'd seen both on television in preparation for this weekend. One had worked on some great baking show in England as a guest judge and had her own Netflix series where she taught home cooks the basics with a sort of "everyone can cook" attitude. The other had his own shows on prime-time TV, where he yelled mercilessly at people. They even had to put up a "strong language" warning before each of his shows. And though he's French, his command of English curses was admirable.

Laila didn't need dossiers on these two. She had memorized the judges' loves and hates like they were player stats and she was betting all her allowance on the Super Bowl.

Philippa, at the closest workstation to me, swept a glossy strand of blond hair behind her ear. "Oh my gosh. It's him. It's Chef Remi," she whispered. Not quietly enough, though, because I heard her loud and clear.

At first I thought it was awe on her face. Then I saw the pinch of her eyebrows. Another emotion, unnameable, lay just under the surface.

But the sugary-sweet "Welcome, y'all!" of the thin, older white woman with silver Betty White curls brought out a smile in everyone. We all greeted her back, even Jaden, who for once looked interested in someone other than himself.

"I'm Chef Polly Rose, and I am so tickled to be judging the work of you talented young folks," she said, clasping her hands in front of her. Her signature charm bracelet, with miniature cake slices and cookie charms dangling from it, circled her petite wrist. "This weekend is going to be so much fun, I promise you."

Where she was bubbles, Chef Remi was a brick. "Fun?" Something about the sneer on his face made us feel guilty for having been enjoying ourselves moments earlier. Like when someone cool says that flare jeans are out of style and there you are, in all your flare-legged glory. As quickly as the smiles bloomed, they withered.

"You are not here to have fun. You," he said, eyeing each of the competitors, "are here to win."

LAILA'S JOURNAL ENTRY

Look, in order to understand my feelings at the exact moment when Chef Remi came in, you have to know the backstory. You have to know that this was the moment I'd been preparing my entire life for—okay, the last few months—and why it was so important to win. Here goes.

Lucy and I met on the second day of kindergarten at the playground. She was sitting under a tree with a stack of picture books. She was underlining phrases with a pencil and nodding to herself. I thought that was weird. I thought she was weird, as did most of the other kids, which is why I kept my distance from her on the first day. But then, after thinking about it, I realized I was weird too, so why not be weird together?

I walked across the playground with my lunch box

and sat down beside her. She sniffed like she was allergic to my presence, or to the many blooming flowers that were behind us, who could tell. She adjusted her baby frames on her face, and I decided that she was in desperate need of something delicious.

I shoved an extra cupcake from my lunch box in her hand. I packed my own lunches and I liked to bring something yummy in case the day called for it. And this was one of those "in case" moments.

She didn't ask what it was, only said thank you and unwrapped it before taking the biggest bite I'd ever seen a person take of a cupcake. We both laughed. She had frosting on her cheek.

She said, "I'm Lucy."

I said, "I'm Laila."

And that was it. We became best friends. Look out, world! Laila and Lucy were an inseparable team of awesomeness.

When Dad died, she was at the funeral and swung beside me at the park across the street in our black clothes. When her parents renewed their vows, I was there in a flowery dress, throwing lilacs with Lucy before they walked down the aisle. When that jerk kid Brian McClusky told Lucy that she and her parents should go back to their own country, I pushed him and told him this was her country. And when some kids pulled my curly hair and called me names, Lucy informed them that she had filed a complaint with their parents and teachers on my behalf, though speaking up made her uncomfortable. They never messed with us again.

But when she joined the journalism club, and I did after-school cooking classes, we both worried we'd become too different to hang out. We were worried we'd drift apart.

Then one afternoon, Lucy came over to stream the latest season of The Great British Bake Off on Netflix—and an ancient movie called Harriet the Spy—while we gobbled snacks and made plans for the future. All those worries about breaking the dream team were only worries.

While I cooked and baked, she parked at the kitchen table and worked on stories for the school newspaper. When I was researching cookbooks after school at the library, she'd sit in the stacks doing her homework and sometimes pepper me with study questions for our upcoming tests.

When Sunderland Academy announced the Golden Cookie contest and I breezed through the qualification round, she wanted to strategize. This was the only way we could remain together when the public school district lines wanted to rip us apart. It's not that Lucy and I can't live without each other, it's just that, why should we? Which is why when Chef Remi said we came here to win, I completely agreed.

Failure wasn't an option.

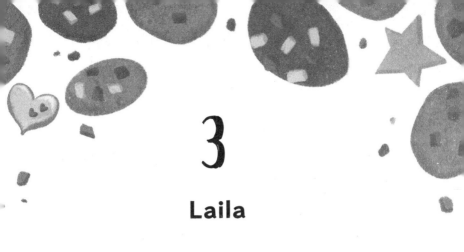

3

Laila

PICTURE IT: THE benches were loaded with ingredients and everyone stood there on pins and needles waiting for the first challenge to drop. Chef Remi scowled, which was sorta his normal look: resting scowl face. He was taller than I imagined, and his expertly styled blond hair marbled with strands of gray made him look a lot older than I imagined too. He was also fairly fit for someone who lived and breathed food, and his chef whites were the kind that were custom-made from one of those Brooklyn hipster clothing stores that normal folk can't afford. Ultrachic while being functional. One day, I'd have my own too.

Anyway, I was a huge fan. Sure, I didn't want him to curse at me like he did to the cheftestants on his shows, but I was somewhat certain he wouldn't. I mean, cursing at a bunch of schoolkids would look bad, right?

Meanwhile, Chef Polly was the epitome of southern belle charm, complete with her delicate charm bracelet. Her smile was as sweet as peach pie. Her hair was as fluffy as clouds of meringue.

It occurred to me then that I was hungry. My nerves were too intense that morning to eat, and I thought they'd feed us before the first challenge. But nope, I was wrong. And there was nothing worse than baking when your tummy was angry with you and felt entitled to a little love and care.

With a deep breath, I tried to not think about food or my rivals or the judges or the cameras positioned around the room, broadcasting us to Sunderland admin and parents. I cut a glance at Lucy as she took a seat behind the judges' table and jotted something down in her notebook. Her presence calmed my nerves a bit.

While she sat by watching everything with a sharp eye and questioned Noah, I knew I had to win this competition. For both of us. With her in the same room believing in me, I felt like I could too.

Which was exactly what I was thinking when Chef Remi glowered at us. "Hello? Are you all awake? Do you see me? Can you hear me?"

We looked up at him and said, "Yes, Chef," as loud as we could.

"Good, finally," he muttered, shaking his head. I bet he

wanted to curse at us. "For your first challenge today, we're going to get technical. Underneath each bin in the cubby is a tiny box with a filled chocolate truffle. Taste it, figure out its flavors, and make the most ambitious, complicated, exhausting cookie recipe you've got in your arsenal to match it within two hours. I want to see a mastery of technique, something extraordinary. And I swear, if you're thinking of making a chocolate chip cookie, don't bother unpacking."

There was a slight cough from Chef Polly. "What Chef Remi means is that *we* want to see something that excites you and makes you proud of yourself. I certainly won't begrudge anyone for making a chocolate chip cookie, as long as they do some unusual, out-of-the-box twists we've never seen before and match the flavor profile of the bonbon. Okay?" She gave us one of her heart-melting smiles that made us—or maybe only me—feel like we were getting a warm hug from our grandma. "And just so you know, you're already here. We are already impressed. We want to see what you've got."

Chef Remi gave her a look that reminded me of a torch scorching a crème brûlée. There was hatred seeping from his pores like garlic after you eat one too many garlic naans— even though it's totally worth it.

I tried not to let his waves of negativity wash over me as I—and the others—grabbed the tiny paper box below the bench. There was a sticker on top featuring the brand of

Chef Remi's bakery in L.A. called Sweet Hélène. *Oooo.* For a few seconds, all I heard was the sound of ripped paper and slight gasps as everyone tore their boxes open. When I looked inside, I saw a tiny white truffle—a bonbon, as Chef Polly called it—with yellow edges. Without needing to taste it, I knew it was white chocolate and some kind of citrus mix. I picked it up, marveling at the shininess of the chocolate coating. I gulped. This was going to be delicious. I popped the confection in my mouth and chewed slowly. As I had thought before, it was citrus. Specifically lemon. But that wasn't all . . . there was an airiness to it. Something delicate and frothy. Something very easily missed.

My superpower senses tingled with the answer. A smile spread across my cheeks. Funny I'd thought about meringue earlier, because that was exactly the recipe I needed to make to match my truffle. My lemon meringue cookies. Firm lemon cookies with a soft, cake-like crumb (courtesy of sour cream, cream cheese, and now a dollop of white chocolate), a tangy lemon curd that I'd spoon in the hollowed-out center, and a velvety meringue to top it all off. And then torched like Chef Remi's gaze.

Would it be exhausting? Yes. But would it win me the challenge? You betcha!

I took off through the kitchen, scrambling to get my ingredients, when I collided with Jaden. He was a few inches taller than me, but his bright green eyes pinned me in place.

"Stay out of my way, cheater. You and your *bestie* shouldn't even be here."

"Seriously? You're accusing me of cheating, again?" I jutted my chin out and gave him the most "I'll stomp your butt" glare I could muster. "I get it. I beat you at Fable Creek Apple Fest and I hurt your feelings. But I don't cheat. I win. Don't cry too hard when you lose like you did last time."

He scoffed and attempted to say something when I stepped around him and scuttled to the walk-in. I opened the door, taking a moment to shake off any nervous anger Jaden brought out of me. While it was true that I beat him at the apple pie competition last fall, it was by a single point. One of the judges was our town librarian and she *maybe* showed a bit of favoritism to me.

Maybe.

Anyway, the whole thing made me doubt my place at the Golden Cookie, which was why I needed a breather in the walk-in. Yet when I looked inside, there stood Philippa and Maeve, deep in conversation. When they saw me, they jumped apart like I'd caught them up to no good.

Wait. This is probably one of those details Lucy would want me to elaborate on. She'd tell me to slow down and figure out what I saw, from their facial expressions to how they were acting, because this could be important.

I didn't hear them talking, but Philippa looked heated: her cheeks were a bright pink, which might've been from the cold. Maeve rubbed her long-sleeved arms—she donned what she called her lucky lab coat instead of an apron like the rest of us—either to maintain warmth or because she was nervous. They looked like they were . . . I don't know, maybe arguing? Neither of them seemed to be getting ingredients—though Philippa was clutching something small in her hand—and neither of them seemed to want to leave the walk-in either. The whole thing was weird, but I didn't have time for anything other than my cookies.

I wriggled by them quickly to find lemons, sour cream, cream cheese, and butter, noticing a slightly open bag of almond flour with a soft grayish tint. Which briefly made me think that I should check my own ingredients to see if anything else was bad, but I didn't want to waste another minute in here, considering how tensely Maeve and Philippa stared at me. So without waiting for them to explain or leave, I took my ingredients and bolted right back to my bench. There, I could focus on my craft and beat all these people.

The clock read eighty-five minutes left of the challenge. *Right.* I'd begun creaming my butter and granulated sugar when Noah came over. He was overly friendly and polished—well, except for his shaggy black hair that definitely needed some time with a brush.

"What are you making for us today?"

After a quick glance at Lucy, who watched everything from her perch across the kitchen, I put on my best smile. My hands twitched by my sides. I was nervous, yet there was no reason I should have been. I deserved to be there. Yes, the other contestants were talented and came from rich families, but I'd spent all my time perfecting this craft. I won the qualification round. I was just as talented.

And I would prove it.

"I'm making lemon meringue cookies. They'll be a nice balance of sweet and tangy—especially with my homemade extract, and I think the judges will enjoy my unique spin on a classic flavor combo."

Noah's grin was wide as he responded. "I'm sorry I'm only now meeting you for the first time. There was a mix-up at the admissions office. They . . . uh, had selected towns that were more . . . likely and—and more equipped to send students to Sunderland. Regardless, it would seem someone on the support staff set up a qualifier round in Fable Creek and forgot to inform me. I'd only seen the other four contestants' rounds, and I had no idea you'd be joining us until the very last minute."

"Huh," I said, unwrapping the cream cheese. I didn't like the implication that I was a last-minute choice of a contestant because I came from a poor town and there was a mistake in the admissions office. But this event was live streaming, and I knew from baking show competitions that you are always supposed to talk excitedly for the cameras so people knew to root for you. I tried to keep my response light. "I thought there was always supposed to be five of us?"

"No, but we are very happy to have you here." His eyes roved elsewhere as the other contestants stood at their benches, creating masterpieces I would have to beat, yet he stayed with me. Then he met my gaze. "Now, I'm supposed to walk around and make conversation, but I wanted you to know that you are welcome here. We are grateful you are sharing your talents with us. Good luck, Laila." He leaned in and dropped his voice to a whisper. "I'm rooting for you."

My heart beat a little stronger and I thanked him before he bounced over to Micah the Mighty, who was whipping his egg whites by hand because he was *that* powerful. I didn't care, though. I had so much work to do and not enough time. Still, Noah's words sank in a little. I wasn't really supposed to be there . . . but then he was rooting for me. If I thought about the first part too much, I'd second-guess everything.

Yet the second part gave me confidence to keep going. Noah believed in me. Lucy believed in me. My dad always believed in me. I could do this.

Thirty minutes later, I'd finished my lemon curd and scooped my cookie dough. I was feeling good and on schedule. Everything was done just the way I liked it, and after a few samples, I knew I'd win with these cookies. With my head held high, I strutted across the room to put my lemon cookies into the carousel oven: one massive oven that rotates trays around like a carousel and takes up a lot of space but makes sure all your baked goods bake evenly. My cookies were the first and only ones in there, I noted with pride. As I stood by the oven, I noticed Chef Remi and Chef Polly having an agitated, hand-waving exchange.

I tiptoed a little closer to hear what was going on.

Chef Remi was complaining about this—I think the competition—being beneath him and a huge waste of time. Chef Polly was saying that we, the contestants, were the future, and what better way to be inspired than by watching the next generation of chefs take up the mantle.

Chef Remi responded with a string of curses that I didn't know a person *could* string together.

Chef Polly threw her hands up. "Someday soon you'll become obsolete like I nearly did. Learn your place, be gracious, and try to defy it. Or you'll just . . . Your career . . . will just . . . It will die with you." And with that, she stormed off, but not before proffering big, "everything's okay" smiles to us competitors as she went.

Chef Remi's eyes found mine. I looked away sharply, but I didn't do it soon enough. He came over and slid open the oven door. He stared daggers at my tray of cookies.

"Tan blobs. How inspiring." His droll words cut through my confidence. He slammed the door shut and once again, early in the morning, I was left standing there completely unsure of myself. Which was exactly when Micah strode up.

On instinct, I opened the oven for him and hit the button, stopping the carousel so he could insert his tray of red cookies inside. When he noticed my questioning glance, he smiled and I think my heart pounded so hard, it might've burst from my chest if it weren't so heavily padded.

"Thanks." His hand swooped in front of me, grazing my arm in the process. And wow. So firm. "Red velvet cookies."

"Ah," I think I squeaked. "Really cool." And although they seemed perfectly formed and probably tasty, I wouldn't have made those. The combo was classic, but the execution was a problem . . . and I was surprised. He should have made a sweet cream cheese insert so that when the cookie was cut, it'd be oozy and gooey perfection. After all, he was the same contestant that made those ginger cookies from the van that were complex, traditional flavors with an untraditional spin. Those cookies would've been hard to beat, while these were too simple.

I knew he was better than this, so why wasn't he baking like it?

"I don't think I actually introduced myself earlier. I'm Micah. You're Laila, right?" He sidled up to me, and I was worried I might die. Like breathing in the same space as Micah the Mighty would cause my brain to stop working and I'd fall over, taking down bins of sugar and flour in the process. People would have called it death by smoldering. Worse, up close he was more beautiful, way more smolder-ish. Which I was not thinking at that moment really, because I knew in about two minutes my cookies would be done, and my lemon curd, currently sitting in the blast chiller, would have to come out.

To be polite, I would have to respond. "Argh eh?"

"I'm sorry?" Micah asked. "What did you say?"

"Laila, that's me." Those were the words that left my mouth. Like, I could've said anything, but that's what I said. "Anyway. Nice to see you. Eat you. Meet you! I mean, I look forward to eating your cookies, not eating you. I gotta go."

And I almost left without taking my cookies from the oven. But my brain was smarter than my mouth, so I took my tray out with my pot-holdered hands and gave him a cringey look that was supposed to be a lovely, normal smile. Of course that didn't work out.

When I got back to my bench, I set the cookies down

and ran to get my lemon curd from the blast chiller. Mortification rolled off me. On a less important day, I might've needed a break. Yet today was no ordinary day.

No one, no matter how pretty, would distract me from my goal: win at all costs.

So I got to work. Using a melon baller, I scooped out a precise circle of each cookie's innards and replaced it with a healthy scoop of lemon curd. Once those were finished, I shoved them into the walk-in and set off to make the most velvety meringue anyone had ever tasted.

And I succeeded. Once I put my egg whites, a pinch of cream of tartar, a quarter cup of sugar, and a bit of sea salt into a bain-marie—a double boiler on the stove top—the magic began. With my thermometer and whisk, I brought the mixture up to—

Okay, I know, I KNOW, these aren't the kind of details Lucy meant when she said we needed to write down everything that happened. I know that writing about how I made the best meringue ever isn't going to help her write her scholarship-worthy portfolio pieces and I should get back to describing what everyone else was doing. But I disagree. I think everyone should know how to make an incredible meringue.

Besides, I'm not entirely sure where the judges and

Noah were or what the other contestants were doing other than baking.

I was so busy—what with all the pressure weighing heavy on me to succeed and all—I didn't see what was really happening until it was too late. Attempted murder. Calculated, brutal attempted murder. Ooof, writing about it gives me the chills. I can only remember the cookie crumbles everywhere.

Maybe Lucy had a better, less distracted view of the kitchen. She wants to be the one who tells the story anyway.

She hasn't looked up from her journal for almost ten minutes—she must be on to something.

LUCY'S JOURNAL ENTRY

First of all, Chef Polly didn't actually storm off. Philippa and Maeve wouldn't stop looking at each other. They were plotting something, and I'm determined to find out what.

I may have come here to write about a cookie competition, but I've found something better. Well, better for my scholarship application. Not better because there was an attempted murder.

So if I blow this crime wide open and write a stellar, hard-hitting piece on it? That's just what Ariella Wilborn would do. It would be exactly the kind of writing sample Tonya said my application was missing.

Problem is, we don't have any clue who the potential murderer may be. I'm going to have to dig out those dossiers I made for Laila and beef them up. I'll take a look at them after Laila goes to sleep, though.

I don't want her seeing the one I made on her.

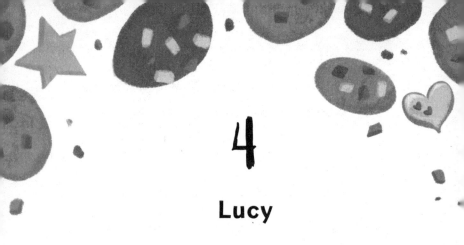

4

Lucy

WATCHING THE COMPETITORS made me realize that all our baking show marathons were missing a key element: the smell.

I concentrated on jotting every detail down for the piece that would serve as both my school paper article and my scholarship application writing sample: the who, what, when, where, and why. After snapping a few photos of the competitors in action, I even sketched a diagram of the kitchen. I mapped out everything from where the judges sat, to where Jaden looked like he hadn't blinked for almost two minutes, to where Laila and Micah were practically waltzing around the ovens with their cookie sheets. But I was almost at a loss for words for how delicious the cookies smelled, how scents of chocolates and citrus and sugar floated into the air as the cookies baked. How was I supposed to wow the scholarship committee with my writing if I kept using words like *good* and *yummy*? I needed to show that I could do more than the simple, boring pieces jerk editor in chief Peter assigned me, and the first step was dusting off these sensory detail skills.

A loud conversation by the double doors distracted me. Chef Polly wanted to leave the kitchen, mid-round.

Noah planted himself between her and the doors. "I'm sorry, Chef Polly, but the kind folks at the Golden Cookie Foundation made the rules crystal clear when they appointed me the coordinator. Both judges must be present for the entire round."

Chef Polly's face stayed its perfect, grandma-y shade of pleasantness. Anyone else would assume she was unbothered, but I homed in on the tippity-tapping of her flamingo-pink loafer: she was annoyed. "But honey, surely a quick trip to the ladies' room would be allowed?"

Noah shook his head, and I had to admire the guy's adherence to the rules. He had no problem saying no to Chef Polly, one of the biggest TV chefs out there.

It took all my nerve to say no to Peter for the school dance—Laila had to butt in with a "What part of 'no' do you not understand, Peter?" for me when I'd responded to his question too quietly—and look where that got me. Being a journalist gave me a reason to ask people questions. I got to dig into people's lives in a way that I wouldn't socially.

But self-doubt bred self-doubt—I read that on a wall hanging in a discount store. Not standing up to a grudge-holding editor in chief meant that I didn't sharpen my skills as much as I'd wanted to on all those shallow stories. I wasn't a bad journalist: I just needed a chance to write some different kinds of pieces to show how good I was.

So when Laila got a spot in the Golden Cookie Competition, we convinced the student newspaper adviser to assign the story to me, completely sidestepping Peter. It worked, and now I was here at Sunderland, watching these esteemed chefs unveil their diva sides.

Since kindergarten, Laila has been around to boost me up and, when necessary, stick up for me when I hesitated to do it myself. Being here at the competition gave me a chance to cheer her on too: I didn't know why she doubted herself when she was literally the best baker I knew. Hopefully she'd finally accept that after she read the "Laila Thomas: A Force with Flour" profile I was finishing up.

But the drama between Chef Polly and Noah drew my attention away from the baking.

"There's only ten minutes left in this round," Noah said to Chef Polly. "The foundation chairpeople may be monitoring via the live stream, but it'll take me longer than that to have them vote on permission for you to leave."

"All right. But I'm going to make a phone call. Is there

anything in the rules about that?" Chef Polly's voice was sweet as pecan pie, and I nearly missed the white-knuckled grip she had on her cell phone. Years of being on camera must have trained Chef Polly well in frosting over her emotions.

My ability to read people was why the teacher adviser for the school newspaper loved my work: I didn't miss those little details that signaled big changes in emotional states.

Noah smiled, but he didn't move from his spot in front of the doors. "Go right ahead, Chef."

Chef Polly stomped away, already dialing. Meanwhile, Chef Remi had made his way over to where Laila was filling a pastry bag with her meringue. The contestants he'd already visited—Philippa and even arrogant Jaden—looked like a herd of bulls had stampeded through their stations, and they were barely recovering. Philippa, flushed as pink as Chef Polly's shoes, dabbed a sleeve against her wet eyes. Chef Remi had made a middle schooler cry.

Seeing him stalk toward Laila, focused and clearly happy at her work, made me want to scream out a warning like it was a horror movie happening in slow motion. My profile on her was supposed to highlight her talent, complete with a smiley photo of her hoisting up the Golden Cookie trophy. That might not happen if Chef Remi crushed her confidence like he did the other contestants.

The chef peered down at the bowl in Laila's arms. "That lemon curd. It's the color of a melted rubber duckie."

My heart squeezed at the sight of Laila's shoulders drooping ever so slightly. The excitement in her eyes dimmed.

"With all due respect, I don't control the color of the lemons you give us."

Chef Remi didn't bother responding before going to ruin the next competitor's mood.

There wasn't a happy face left in the room by the time Chef Remi crossed it. Then the man had the nerve to stroll right back to the judges' table through the central aisle, as if he wanted one last look at the dejected faces he'd left in his wake. For a moment, we made eye contact. I thought he was going to chew me out too, but then he proceeded to drop into his chair without the barest acknowledgment of my existence.

I stared down at my notebook for the next few minutes, trying to organize my notes to see what other vivid, enriching details I could add that weren't about how stressed or gloomy the contestants seemed. My soundtrack was the clang of kitchenware, the annoyed whispering of Chef Polly wrapping up her phone call, and, finally, Noah announcing a five-minute warning and telling the competitors to put their finishing touches on their work.

I didn't realize it was humanly possible for the competitors to move faster, but the kitchen broke out in a flurry of activity. Micah's arms flexed as he piped the finishing touches—tiny green globs that looked like succulents—onto his red velvet. Maeve whimpered when one of her cookies broke while she was transferring it to a plate. A bead of sweat rolled down Laila's temple as she set down her torch.

Noah called time, and there was a collective exhale as the competitors let that pent-up tension leave their bodies. No wonder Chef Polly thought that this shared nerve-racking experience would bond everyone. The bakers looked like extras on a superhero movie set, surveying the damage after the big alien invasion.

I rose from my stool to snap a few photos of the relieved competitors and their work before the chefs broke their hearts even more. Noah roamed the kitchen, whispering some encouraging words along the way and somehow managing to get Philippa to dry her tears. Chef Polly beamed and thanked each competitor. Chef Remi glowered and stayed silent. He must've been saving up his energy for the cookie critique—or, more accurately, criticism, because the man had a creative way of telling each person how awful he thought their work was.

According to Chef Remi, Maeve's cookies were dry, like a mouthful of sand from the playground, which was where she belonged. She gave a curt "Thank you, Chef" anyway.

Her hand stayed wrapped tight around the thin blade she'd used to craft the tiny gum-paste doves adorning her cookies.

He then called Philippa's work bland. Actually, it was worse than that. He said, "I'd call this baby food, but that would be an insult to babies' taste buds."

The tears resurfaced in Philippa's eyes, and as soon as Chef Remi sauntered away, she yanked off her apron. A glint of metal caught my gaze. Philippa had brought her own sheathed chef's knife to hand-chop the pistachios in her cookie. It had a white marble handle with a gold *PW* etched into it, different from the black- and wood-handled knives here. But bringing any outside materials was against the rules. Laila had to go through a whole approval process to bring her extracts because Sunderland wouldn't have them. I had even helped her write her request. The competition folks drew the line at her lucky whisk. So how had Philippa managed it?

Chef Remi then moved on to Micah, who at thirteen stood only a couple of inches shorter than the chef. Micah's imposing stature didn't seem to bother him one bit, because Chef Remi practically shouldered him aside to get to Micah's plate.

Micah crossed his arms, and those arms tensed when Chef Remi leveled his insult at him: uninspired. Despite Chef Polly calling the red velvet cookies some of the best she'd ever tasted, Chef Remi said they were far too safe a choice for a competition of this caliber and as ambitionless as his cousin Horace. None of us even understood that reference, but the tone told us Horace Boucre was not known in his family for overachieving. For a kid experienced in baking competitions like this, shouldn't Micah have strategized better about how to impress the judges?

The most positive thing Chef Remi said was that Jaden's puff pastry cardamom palmiers did not reek of teenage-boy body wash like he'd expected. That didn't keep Jaden from palming the kitchen shears as Chef Remi strolled away.

But then he got to Laila, and I instinctively drew closer: a protective measure, given how she'd reacted to him earlier. I don't know that there's anything I could've physically done to have her back, but Laila smiled at me nervously like she sensed how hard I was rooting for her. Honestly, she probably didn't need to look at me for support: we always have each other's backs.

Chef Polly picked up one of Laila's meringues, daintily, with a pinkie out. "My, aren't these lovely! Just like your polka-dot apron."

"Thank—"

"I don't think either is particularly lovely," Chef Remi cut in, "though perhaps, in fashion, success is more subjective. One person's trash can be another's treasure."

I made a face so that Laila didn't have to.

While Chef Remi was busy being snarky, Chef Polly had taken a nibble of Laila's lemon meringue cookies. The corners of her lips curved up into a smile. "Well done, Laila. You've got the perfect level of tartness in there. It makes every single bite interesting. And this meringue? You really matched the cookie to the bonbon, down to that sneaky little meringue."

Laila thanked Chef Polly graciously while I bit back a squeal. They weren't supposed to have an audience at this competition, let alone a cheerleader, so I needed to keep myself in the background. I scribbled down the word *tartness* in my notes. It'd be a welcome addition to the generic *good*s and *yummy*s I had down.

Chef Remi sniffed—*sniffed*—the cookie before tasting it. He set it down after one bite. "Chef Polly, I don't agree with your taste in fashion, nor do I apparently agree with your taste in cookies. I simply don't see what, in this competitor's work, you're impressed by."

In fifth grade, Laila baked an edible birthday card for the most popular girl in school. When we spotted it untouched in the cafeteria trash moments after she gifted it, Laila's brows pinched together in confusion first, then her mouth went ajar. She'd said, very quietly, "Oh," that one syllable the sound of her soul letting its dreams go.

And that was exactly how she sounded when she responded to Chef Remi.

"Oh."

I would've chucked the school's DSLR camera right at Chef Remi's head if it wouldn't have gotten Laila and me immediately ejected—and if I hadn't signed all those liability forms. He hadn't had the decency to insult Laila to her face: he'd spoken to Chef Polly instead.

"But, if I had to choose who did the best," Chef Remi continued with disdain, "I suppose I'd have to pick unimpressive Laila over uninspired Micah, unappetizing Philippa, unexceptional Jaden, and unimaginative Maeve. Congratulations, Laila, on being the least worst. You will receive no advantage in the next round but an acknowledgment that your work was satisfactory when we consider today's winner."

And with that, as Laila recovered her senses enough to offer a sincere-sounding "Thank you, Chef," Chef Remi strolled out of the room as if he had somewhere better to be. Chef Polly took an extra moment to commend the competitors for their work. Then she scurried out the double doors too, probably beelining for the ladies' room visit she was denied earlier.

Noah, the apology plain on his face, overcompensated

with his cheerfulness when he spoke. "Whew, what a whirl-wind of a first round! You all did splendidly, especially our last-minute entry, Laila!"

Last-minute entry? Embarrassment flickered across Laila's face so quickly that anyone other than a best friend would've missed it. Even if Noah was trying to compliment her, it came off a little insulting, like she was different from everyone. Like the way people threw around the saying "You're one of the good ones," which actually implied that everyone else like you were bad ones. Given Noah's role as coordinator, though, Laila probably didn't feel as confident as she usually did about speaking up.

Jaden snorted. "Your boss didn't seem to think any of us did well, even her."

Noah dismissed the thought with a casual wave. The movement looked too easy, too second nature, like he was used to explaining for his employer. "That's just his way. It's part of his television persona, and he has to keep up appearances. Trust me, when I go check in with him and Chef Polly on the scores, he'll have nothing but positive things to say about you all."

Noah's smile lingered a second too long: he was lying. And even if I hadn't caught that tiny tell of his, it was unlikely, after Remi's behavior earlier, that the chef was as sweet and gooey on the inside as Noah was claiming.

"Feel free to leave your things here and head down the hall for lunch," Noah said. "Be back in an hour. We'll begin round two. It may sound like Laila has an edge, but it's anyone's game and I can't wait to announce the day one's winner."

Jaden wadded up his apron and tossed it on the bench. "If there is one."

"Someone has to be, right?" Maeve asked.

Philippa headed for the door. "If you believe Chef Remi, we're all equally losers. Humph. Tell that to my family and our millions."

"Well, I'm going to skip lunch. I want to check on my plant and try to get in a run," Micah said.

A rumble shook the windows then, and we all paused and glanced outside.

"Looks like a storm's coming in," I said.

Jaden clapped his hands. "Meteorologist of the Year right there. Give that girl a Pulitzer."

Laila threaded her arm through mine. "Ignore him. We've got to scarf down lunch and strategize. Chef Remi may not have been impressed by my lemon meringue cookies this time, but I guarantee that my round-two work is going to knock him dead."

LAILA'S JOURNAL ENTRY

The end of everything normal began at lunch. We were all in sour moods, some of us might've wanted sweet revenge, and worse . . . someone almost succeeded.

But it wasn't me—despite what everyone thinks. I only wanted to bake my heart out.

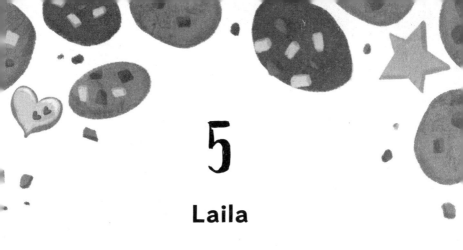

5

Laila

WHEN WE ENTERED the school cafeteria, I could barely keep my eyes from bulging out of my head. It was all polished dark wood, filled with large antique-looking circular tables and their matching seats with emerald-green-cushioned bottoms. It was fancy—not like our wobbly long tables with plastic benches on dented linoleum back home.

No, this place was where rich people ate regularly and never thought twice about it.

There were empty canisters along the back wall that I assumed were usually stuffed with cereal, and different stations on both ends of the room where I imagined there were cafeteria workers ready to fill plates with delicious, custom-made meals. Unfortunately, no one was manning those when we stepped inside.

"Huh. Aren't there any staff here besides Noah and the

judges?" I wondered. There was something slightly off that we were alone in this massive school for the big competition. Sure, the event was live streamed, but no one else was here outside of it.

Lucy leaned in. "I've been wondering about that too. I wanted to ask if they had oat milk, but I haven't found any food service staff. There should at least be someone prepping meals in between challenges, right? Or maintenance. . . ."

"Hm," I mumbled. "Well, big celebrities like Chef Remi and Chef Polly definitely wouldn't dedicate their time to something that was disorganized."

Lucy gave a thoughtful nod. "And maybe because there are so few of us, the school didn't think they needed anyone else around to babysit or dust bookshelves or whatever."

"Right. More staff means more money, and tuition here is already way too high." I let my shoulders ease down. It all made sense. "Anyway, I need to strategize and eat."

I focused on the two tables in the center of the room, where there were six massive pizzas: pepperoni, vegetable, plain cheese, and Hawaiian pies—which only Jaden ate, further emphasizing he was suspicious. Pineapple on pizza is a crime only a villain would commit.

Lucy and I took our paper plates, filled them with vegetable and cheese slices, and sat at our own table together. We shouldn't have been so chummy since the other competitors already thought we were somehow cheating . . . but I was in a mood.

Although I had won the round, Chef Remi had managed to crush my dreams and make me doubt everything. I didn't come from money or a well-connected family restaurant like the others. It made me wonder if I was the underdog who would never truly fit in. . . .

The only thing I was certain of, at that moment, was that if I shoved warm, cheesy pizza in my mouth, I'd be less hungry. Besides, Lucy would get me back on track. Lucy would know the right thing to say. She always did.

But before she could start her pep talk, Philippa and Maeve took seats beside us at the table. There were a million (okay, twenty-something) tables, and they decided to sit with us? Ugh. Philippa only had a bottle of water and a sneer on her face.

"I can't believe you're eating that." She sniffed, looking disdainfully at our pizza. "Uninspired, barely any toppings, the cheapest pizza off campus—and it's cold. They invite us here to make amazing food and they can't provide us with a healthy variety? My mom's going to rage."

Meanwhile, Maeve nibbled on her own pepperoni. "It's not that bad and I'm sure you're hungry."

Philippa's face softened. "I guess you're right. We need to eat if we want to keep up our strength. And what Mom doesn't know . . ." She rose and darted off for a plate and pizza, leaving Lucy, Maeve, and me alone.

Lucy coughed, glancing my way before turning to Maeve. She wanted me to play nice with my fellow competitors. She knew how focused I could be on winning. Or in this case, thinking about pizza.

"Did you two know each other before the competition today?" she asked Maeve.

I recognized Lucy's tone, the sugary-sweet one she uses to pester people for information without them realizing it. She must've noticed something about the other two girls, maybe something that could give me a competitive edge. I'd ask her later.

"Me and Philippa?" Maeve set her pizza on the plate. "Hmmm, yeah. We met a few times at a . . . a club after school."

"What club?" I asked carefully. She seemed shy, a bit hesitant to share anything with us, despite her sitting at our table.

Maeve's mouth opened and then whooshed shut when Philippa took a seat beside her with a plate of vegetable pizza. She blotted the oil with a napkin, as if that were going to make it magically healthier. I refrained from shaking my head.

"How do you think round one went?" Philippa didn't

seem to care that we were already in the middle of a conversation.

"Chef Remi was brutal," I admitted. The others had dealt with the chef's cruelty too. Being up-front about it meant that, yeah, this was a competition, but we had something in common, something to bond over, like Chef Polly said.

"Brutal to you because you have thin skin and zero talent," Jaden shouted two tables over.

Philippa laughed at—not with—him, cutting through the tension quickly. "I saw Chef Remi spit your cookie out the moment he turned away from you. At least he ate Laila's."

Jaden scowled and busied himself with his paper plate.

Maeve elbowed Philippa in the ribs, and her voice dropped to a whisper. "Don't poke the bear. He's good, and when he's riled up, he might get better." Maeve plucked a green pepper off Philippa's pizza and gobbled it. The two shared a quick smile.

That's when I started to think they knew each other better than meeting a few times at a club. Who ate off a stranger's plate like that? But they were both too . . . mysterious to share how they were friends. Or what they were doing in the walk-in when I went to get my ingredients. Something suspicious was going on—not only with them but with everything—yet I couldn't figure out what.

By chance, my eyes roved over Micah the Mighty (maybe

I shouldn't call him that). Lucy will think this is ridiculous, but . . . I mean the name fits. Anyway, as I was saying, Micah the Mighty was sitting at the edge of the cafeteria pounding slice after slice because he must have been famished or he was stress eating, as I sometimes did when I felt like the weight of the world was on my shoulders. I noticed a few stray leaves of his plant poking from his pocket, and I wondered if it was some herb that made the pizza taste better. When he caught me staring, he gave me a little wave and my entire body nearly burst into flames. I held in a cringe and turned away.

Why didn't Micah sit with the rest of us? Maybe he didn't have friends—*human* friends, at least, since his potted plant was probably sitting in a patch of light in his room—or know how to talk to people. Maybe that's why he wanted to get into Sunderland so bad. . . . He wanted to find friends.

Which was when I realized that I didn't know why any of these contestants wanted to get into Sunderland. Not really. Me and Lucy, sure. But Philippa, Maeve, Micah, Jaden . . . why Sunderland?

My eyes darted to Philippa. "Why do you want to win this competition so bad? Your parents can afford Sunderland, right?"

Lucy shot a wide-eyed "play nice!" glare at me that I ignored. She was the pro at getting information out of people in a friendly way, not me.

Philippa's face twitched, and her chin jutted out. "That's none of your business." The way her shoulders climbed to the tips of her ears made me immediately back off. I got the impression that Philippa was keeping a lot of huge secrets and she wasn't ready to share them with anybody. Except Maeve.

"What about you?" I asked Maeve.

While Philippa was all glowering fury, Maeve was all smiles. "I know my family has a growing ramen-fusion empire and people think we've got it all, but I'm like . . . the fifth kid in my family. All my older siblings go to Ivy Leagues or fancy schools that cost a lot. Mom and Dad can't afford another tuition right now. Anyway, I love Sunderland, and I think it'd be great to go here. Their science decathlon team is the best in the state. You?"

I told her about my mom—not mentioning my dead dad because people tended to treat me differently when I told them that—and about my big dreams. At the end, even Philippa looked a little more sympathetic.

Jaden dumped his plate in the garbage and stopped beside our table. "My father's on the Sunderland Board of Directors already. My older brother, Charlie, goes here. I came here to win, for no other reason." He smirked at me and Lucy. "And I will win. Just watch. I've got day one in the bag."

With that, he took off, leaving us staring after him. I noticed that he patted his pants pocket on the way out and his body sagged in relief, which was odd. But then again, *Jaden* was odd. We finished up our pizza in silence, each of us quietly mulling over how we'd push through the pressure and stress of this competition. Round two was going to be intense. Really not fun at all.

Do I have to write about it? It makes me feel queasy . . . and I don't want to relive it. But Lucy asked me to put down every single non-micah's-arms-related detail for her article and I don't want to let her down.

At first, Lucy came here to write about the cookie competition. I lent her some of my cookbooks so she could learn foodie words to spice up her scholarship application writing sample.

Then she wanted to investigate the event, despite me telling her how bad it would be for me. I get it: if she uncovers the potential murderer and exposes them, it'd be high-profile enough to get her that scholarship for sure. Yet investigating would also put more focus on me . . . especially when she finds out what I did in the walk-in.

Everyone believes it was me. I'm the girl from a poor family from a poor town who would do anything to win, right? People here want me to be guilty. If Lucy kicks up dirt, I'll look the dirtiest somehow.

That said, I'll do this. Which means writing the next, terrible things. Lucy is my only friend in a nest of vipers. I hope she'll drop it. She knows I would never do anything bad; she believes in me. She has to.

Back in the kitchen, aprons tied around our waists, all of us a bit jittery, we waited for the chefs to come and tell us the challenge. We already knew it would be difficult, that's why we were so silent. Even Lucy stared off at nothing while she perched on her stool far away from me.

Noah stood at the head of the room. There was a smile plastered to his face as sweat beaded at the edge of his scalp. His eyes kept shifting from us to the doors, and he kept running his hands down his shirt as if they were coated in something sticky. All of us were terrified, it would seem. Though I couldn't imagine why Noah was scared too. Maybe Chef Remi was meaner in private. I felt bad for him, he seemed like a genuinely nice, well-meaning person stuck with the grumpiest of grumpy chefs for a boss.

We contestants had a huge reason to be afraid: we knew this challenge would set the tone for the rest of the competition. The winner would have a serious leg up for tomorrow. It wouldn't only boost your confidence; it got you a big step closer to winning the whole competition.

And it had to be me. Losing wasn't an option.

When Chef Remi and Chef Polly arrived, they came from different doors on opposite sides of the room. They cast each other glances overflowing with irritation. Chef Polly was one of the most beloved, kindest chefs in the business, and seeing her upset made me feel slightly scared. Yet when she stood in front of the judges' table, she beamed at us all like we were the light of her life. Like our presence made all the darkness disappear everywhere and she was so happy to be there with us.

"The second challenge is going to be a doozy, but I have complete faith in y'all. You can do this!" She pushed a silvery strand behind her ear. "You know how in *The Great British Bake Off,* we do a showstopping showpiece? Well, that's what we're doing today. It's going to be huge! It's going to be fantastic—"

"It's going to be perfect, or you'll be lucky to bake for me ever again," Chef Remi finished with a scowl. "The first round was a disappointment, but Chef Polly reminded me that you are children and prone to making terrible, disgusting mistakes. I hope you'll do better in this challenge." He glared at us, and the pizza churned in my stomach. It felt ten degrees warmer all of a sudden, and I wanted to go hide in the walk-in.

Still, I swallowed my fear and stood taller. Winners didn't cower.

"For this challenge, you will make a cookie showpiece that will have to be at least two feet tall. The taller the better. It's got to be structurally sound and incredibly delicious. Now . . ." Polly gave us a stern look while the corners of her lips lifted as if she couldn't help smiling. "Normally, people would give us gingerbread. But gingerbread is so . . ."

"Passé," Chef Remi said in his very French, very bored accent. "We want cookies that have different flavors, textures, fillings, colors. I want to be wowed."

"We can't wait to see what you come up with!" Chef Polly exclaimed, clapping her hands. "As a bonus, the winner will get to choose the main ingredient for both of tomorrow's challenges. And I don't need to tell you that winning on day one gets you closer to winning the whole kit and caboodle!"

"Now bake!" Noah said chipperly, which did nothing to lessen the pressure in my chest.

I gave a quick look at Lucy, who was already bent over her notepad, and then we set off to work. I could make tall cookie showpieces in my sleep. I'd practiced these a million times. A few of them did topple, yet I was confident in my fairly easy plan. Make and bake three doughs one after the other. If I baked them all at once, with different oven times and temps, that would surely be a way to mess up everything.

No, I had to do this just right.

Triple chocolate filled with white chocolate that would have to be spread out like cake batter and cooked on a full cookie sheet. Brown sugar shortbread made extra hardy with ground oats for all my bases. And last, my trickiest recipe: chocolate chip cookies à la Jacques Torres.

Okay, so maybe you all don't need to know this. But! This is more interesting! Besides, when Lucy realizes that there's nothing more to investigate for her article and to let the detective do his job, she'll need more notes about the actual cookie competition. So why not tell you about my cookie masterpiece? Right?

Anyway, this cookie dough required two different kinds of flour, extremely fancy chocolate disks—not to be confused with the pedestrian chocolate chips—and expensive French butter. My first huge task, then, was to take as much French butter as I could from the walk-in before my competition had the same exact thought.

I flew across the kitchen, noticing that Philippa had a schedule taped to the edge of her bench so she could stay on track. Maeve was using a ruler to draw on parchment so she would have the proper measurements for her cookie pieces. It was very clever. While Micah (the Mighty) was hoarding an absurd amount of molasses for what I assumed would be molasses cookies . . . which wasn't that different from gingerbread. Jaden was out of sight.

Meaning he was likely in the walk-in. I wasn't ready to be around him after what he said at lunch. But I couldn't afford to not go get the butter either.

I decided I'd have to be careful around him and definitely not share my plans or he'd sabotage me, since I seemed to be the person he hated the most.

When I stepped inside, he glanced at me while he was doubled over . . . like he was catching his breath or something. He turned away, suddenly reaching for that grayish almond flour at the same time I reached for the French butter. And then his shoulder collided with mine on purpose.

"Hey," I shouted. "Not cool."

And then he twisted around, crowding my space. "You're a cheater and I'm going to expose you."

I stepped closer to him, our noses almost touching. "I'm tired of you calling me that. Do you think I need to cheat to beat you? News flash—"

"You knew that judge at the apple pie competition. She clearly favored you, I saw it." His lips snarled at me. "You didn't deserve that win then and you won't get one today."

"I didn't cheat." I sniffed, trying not to let his words

get to me. "All of us are good enough to be here, so stop name-calling and bake." I shoved the rancid almond flour into his chest, which was when I noticed he was holding a baggie full of . . . something weird. The color was brownish, so it wasn't powdered sugar, and the baggie's contents were chunky and grainy like ground oats. I sniffed again, this time trying to identify the mysterious substance, but my superpower couldn't pick it out among all the other scents surrounding us. Anyway, it definitely seemed suspect, like it shouldn't be here in the walk-in. Like it was something Jaden pulled out of his pocket, which was doubly suspect given the competition's strict rules.

An episode of Remi's *Kitchen Disasters* came back to me in a flash. "That's not hazelnut, right? Chef Remi's allergic—"

"Everyone knows that." He shoved me into the racks and stalked out, leaving me with my fists clenched by my sides and my chest heaving.

Even though I needed a break to collect my thoughts and shore up my determination, I grabbed the butter and followed him out a second later.

LUCY'S JOURNAL ENTRY

Something isn't adding up about the story Laila is writing in her journal. It's all focused on the nitty-gritty details of her baking and what everyone else was doing.

But it's important to know what she was doing too, isn't it?

And get this: we had the weirdest conversation after I told her I thought she was in the walk-in for a little longer than she'd said.

Laila: Yeah . . . I was calming down. Like I said. Shouldn't you be writing in your own notebook?

Me: I wanted to find out where you were in the story. But you wrote that you didn't have the time to calm down, that you grabbed the butter and left. That's not true.

Laila: You don't believe me?

Me: I'm just trying to get the whole picture here. You were gone for a while. What were you doing? And don't say calming down. I've known you forever and when the worst bullies push your buttons, you don't calm down. You get even.

Laila: If you don't believe me, then I have nothing more to say about it.

Me: I'll write the rest of the story, and you can think about why you don't trust me with your secret.

Laila: Fine.

Me: Fine.

See what I mean?

LAILA'S JOURNAL ENTRY

I'm done writing notes for Lucy because I can't trust my friend to support me. I can't trust her to let things go. All she cares about is the truth, not the person it hurts. This isn't about solving who tried to kill Chef Remi, it's about writing an article that'll get her the scholarship. It's not about friendship anymore, it's about fame. She wants to impress Ariella Wilborn so bad, she'd do anything. Even if it means painting a target on her best friend's back.

6

Lucy

AN HOUR INTO the second round, the competitors were hard at work over their showpieces. Neither of the judges had sat down since they entered the kitchen. Chef Polly strolled around the edges of the room, tapping at her phone screen and pouting. At one point, she was so distracted, she walked straight into Noah, nearly knocking him into Jaden's bench. The cacophony of dishes clattering to the floor and Noah's pockets emptying distracted the competitors, wasting valuable seconds. Meanwhile, Chef Remi paced through the kitchen with a frown that looked like it was carved there.

There was so much movement, but all I did was rewrite my description of what cookie dough looked like for the fifth time. An *Are you sure it's good enough?* floating in my head—in Tonya's voice, of course—made me doubt my words. Restating simple facts, like I was used to, wasn't going to cut it. This piece needed to blow the scholarship committee away. But right now, it wouldn't even blow out a candle.

I was relieved when Noah sat and scooted his stool closer so we could chat. We hunched over our table at the edge of the kitchen. My notebook lay in front of me, my phone—with a frustratingly low connection—next to it. I hoped Noah could provide some extra behind-the-scenes insight into the competition. Or at least some baking-related adjectives I hadn't used yet.

"So, do you have any interest in cooking?" Noah asked me. He must have been feeling an unexciting lull in the round too.

I shook my head. "Journalism is more of my thing. Laila bakes while I reap the rewards."

At her workstation, Laila absentmindedly wiped her hands on her apron. She glanced up first at the clock, then to see where the judges were, then headed toward the walk-in.

Noah smiled. "You two seem like the best of friends."

"We are." I set my pen down. There wasn't a real reason to use it anyway. Rewriting that cookie dough description for the sixth time wouldn't be productive. "How about you and Chef Remi? You've been working together a long time too, right?"

He nodded solemnly, like folks do at church when the priest says something important. "Almost eleven years. He's more of a mentor than a friend, though. He's so respected in the industry. His word will make or break a restaurant. He's even looking at going into business with a not-so-hot ramen place near here, to lend his famous name and bring in clients."

I peered over at Chef Remi then. He was at Maeve's workstation, which was crowded with mixing bowls, spilled ingredients, and dozens of eyedroppers of flavoring extracts. I caught the words "sloppy" and "lazy," and Maeve's lip began to tremble. Chef Remi's face stayed stone-cold.

"He's just one guy. How can he be that important?"

Noah tilted his head as he looked at me. "Is there a reporter you look up to? Whose name do you automatically trust because you know they do good work?"

"Ariella Wilborn, hands down. She did a piece on artificial intelligence and art that should've won a thousand awards."

"Well, Chef Remi is the Ariella Wilborn of baking. I'd bet all the competitors, even your friend Laila, think of him that way. People will drive for hours to go to a Remi restaurant. Him being involved with a restaurant would practically double its revenue overnight."

As if speaking about him summoned him, Chef Remi suddenly appeared next to me.

"Noah, spring water," he ordered, actually snapping his

fingers. "And I must take my heart medication. You picked it up at the pharmacy earlier, no? Or did you bungle that too?"

I cringed on Noah's behalf, though secretly jealous Chef Remi got special water while the rest of us drank bulk store-brand bottles that tasted like rocks.

Noah didn't react to Chef Remi's orders and insults the way I did. Calmly, he pulled an orange bottle of prescription meds from his pocket and a water bottle out of his messenger bag from under the table. He untwisted the caps for the chef, as if the man couldn't be bothered with tamperproof lids. Chef Remi didn't thank him as he swiped the bottles from his hands. Remi chased a pill with a gulp of expensive water.

My mom had always impressed on me the importance of being kind to everyone: classmates, the cafeteria staff, the middle school janitor with his headphones on. I was taught to always say "please" and "thank you," because people will often return the kindness right back at you.

Apparently Chef Remi didn't get that same lesson from his mom or anyone. When he was done with his medicine, he just plopped the open water and pill bottles back on the workstation in front of Noah and marched back toward the competitors. I glanced over at Noah, expecting him to be as put off by the chef's behavior as I was. But Noah's face stayed unbothered, even blank. He didn't seem annoyed that the chef had accidentally spilled a few drops of that expensive water on his forearm. He simply excused himself to grab a towel near the sink.

Most of the rest of round two blurred by with folks whirling around the kitchen arena. Everyone was out of my line of sight at some point.

Halfway through the round, Maeve left the walk-in, juggling a few ingredients in her arms. She dropped an egg but didn't go back to get another one.

That was rude and a little odd that Maeve just left her mess there for someone else to clean up. Maybe it's a rich-kid thing. But why was she in the walk-in if she didn't need ingredients like that egg?

Meanwhile, Jaden disappeared into the walk-in too, after Chef Remi stopped by his station to say something that involved "the technique of a nursery schooler." Jaden practically stomped his way to the walk-in. He came out a couple of minutes later, muttering to himself and death-gripping a carton of heavy whipping cream and a bag of some gray flour.

Philippa was in the walk-in as well, though I didn't notice her go in. I only saw her leave, nearly slipping in the egg that Maeve had dropped.

Micah was the only one who didn't visit the walk-in after his first grab for ingredients, but he did speed back and forth between the oven and his workstation. I didn't see him for a minute, but when he popped up, I realized he was doing push-ups while his cookies were baking.

Noah and Chef Polly wandered from station to station, checking out the cookie doughs, patting backs, politely asking questions, and imparting encouraging words. They were probably trying to counteract Chef Remi's damage.

Even Laila was gone for a while, in the walk-in longer than it took to pick up an ingredient and go.

I was the only one who stayed in one place. Which also meant I was far from any of the action that could help me amp up my application writing samples. A bolder, braver reporter on the school paper might have risked getting in trouble to slink along the walls for better views, better shots with a fancy non-school-owned camera. But Noah had been kind enough to sit with me earlier, and I would've hated to upset him by getting in the way of him and the judges. I stayed at the workstation, with my pen, notebook, and useless phone and Chef Remi's open water bottle.

When the cookies were baked and the ovens were cooling, the contestants were in a tizzy to get their showpieces built on time. It was chaos. Everything seemed louder: tools fell to the floor, sneakers squeaked on the tiles, sheet pans slammed on tables. Everyone's energy ticked up several notches. Chef Polly whizzed through, helping with assembly, all to impress Chef Remi . . . but the judging was as brutal in round two as it was in round one. Philippa's cookies were unremarkable, Chef Remi said. Maeve's cookies belonged in the center—of the trash. Micah's choices were as bland and uncreative as a white crayon.

Chef Remi's mean streak took a nastier turn when he and Chef Polly strolled over to Jaden's station. Jaden had created a nearly four-foot-high tower of macarons, dusted silver and gold so it shimmered in the light.

Chef Polly clasped her hands in front of her. "My, my, this is gorgeous, young man."

Jaden smirked at his fellow competitors.

Chef Remi took a bite of the plated macaron, and as he chewed, I swore I saw a bead of sweat trickle down Jaden's forehead.

"This macaron . . ." We all braced ourselves for his signature brand of meanness. "You know I am French, correct? So why would you possibly think serving me a plate of these abominations of my home cuisine would be a good idea?"

Even Noah cringed like he'd been personally slapped.

Chef Remi went on about the oddly gritty texture, the lackluster filling, something about the "more boring than that other boy's" choice of flavors. The more he spoke, the harder the grimace on Jaden's face set.

By the time the judges got to the last plate, even competition-pro Laila looked frazzled. And this was a girl who looked the vice principal straight in the eye when he accused her of breaking the school dress code and said, "Well then, you're going to have to write up a new dress code, because I look fabulous, and I'm not changing."

As the judges tasted, I leaned forward at my workstation, my elbows on the table, my fingers crossed. Laila had created a three-foot-tall tower, modeled after the solar system—because baking is her whole universe, get it?—of three types of cookies. Compared to Jaden's one type? I was sure Laila was in for a gentler judging.

I barely breathed as Chef Remi bit into chocolate chip cookies à la Jacques Torres.

Chef Polly cut in first, to soften the blow of whatever Chef Remi was sure to say. "You really put a lot of thought and strategy into this piece, I can tell. This shortbread, with the oats? Wonderful."

Laila thanked her, but then the room was silent as everyone turned to Chef Remi. The man was still chewing, that grouchy look on his face.

"Laila, is it?" he asked.

Laila nodded slowly, like she'd gotten in trouble. And maybe she had. "Laila Thomas, Chef."

Chef Remi set down the plate and crossed his arms.

"Right. I want everyone to remember that name. Because Miss Thomas here doesn't belong in this Golden Cookie Competition . . ."

My heart and Laila's broke at the same exact second. But neither of us expected what the world's crankiest chef said next.

". . . because you have more talent than all these other competitors combined. Well done, Miss Thomas. I think you might have what it takes to excel in the culinary world, even at your age."

Jaws around the room dropped. Chef Polly tilted her head like a dog that gets confused when the owner pretends to throw a ball. Chef Remi complimenting someone? Unheard of.

Until today.

Until Laila.

Chef Remi tried the brown sugar shortbread next and dished out some more unexpected praise: "These would give Noah's Scottish mother a run for her money."

The more he spoke, the brighter Laila seemed to shine and the more annoyed the rest of the competitors looked. Meanwhile, I furiously scrawled down quotes word for word for my article. I wanted my surprise profile on my best friend to commemorate every moment of her first-day triumph.

He reached for the last plate, the triple chocolate filled

with white chocolate. These would blow him away: Laila had baked these for my little brother's sixth birthday last year, and that kid is the pickiest eater on this planet.

For a moment, Laila and I locked eyes. I tried to telepathically send all my you-got-this pep talks her way. She smiled and turned back to Chef Remi as he coughed to clear his throat to speak.

But when the chef opened his mouth, nothing came out. Not even a breath. Then his eyes went wide, and his hands grabbed wildly at his throat and chest.

"He's choking!" Laila screeched.

Next to me, Noah vaulted over the workstation. He was behind Chef Remi in two seconds. He wrapped his arms around the chef's waist and started the Heimlich maneuver. But Chef Remi still couldn't breathe.

Chef Polly, the other competitors, and I froze. In our defense, no middle schooler or dainty southern chef looked big enough to wrap arms around the chef to do the Heimlich maneuver like Noah was trying.

Micah, the second-strongest person in the room, looked on, his face blank and his fingers nervously toying with his apron. Jaden took careful steps away until his back was flush against the wall. Philippa and Maeve exchanged unreadable looks, but at least they leaped to catch Chef Polly when she swooned.

I rose off my stool but didn't approach. What could I have done?

"Call 911!" Maeve urged finally.

Laila and I both yanked out our cell phones, only to be reminded how dismal the cellular service at the school was. We cast each other stricken looks. This was an emergency, and we were utterly alone and unable to help.

It was the longest five minutes of my life, and judging by everyone else's faces, it was the same for them.

Eventually, Philippa saw a single bar of cellular service and dialed 911 on Chef Polly's phone as Noah kept up the Heimlich maneuver.

Noah swiped at the sweat pouring down his face as he switched to CPR. One second he was pounding the chef's chest, the next he was listening to his breathing. "Whatever was blocking his windpipe is gone. He's alive, but he's—he's not waking up."

I ran over to Laila and held her hand tight, both of us helpless. Micah clenched his fists around the edge of his workstation. At the wall, Jaden slumped down to a seat on the floor and lowered his forehead onto his knees.

Chef Polly and Maeve began crying. Philippa patted them on their backs, tears pooling in their eyes as she described what was happening to the emergency hotline operator. "Help is on the way," she announced to us.

The room in the air was hot from the ovens, the smells so sweet it almost made me sick. Outside, dark clouds covered the campus, and the fluorescent lights overhead flickered with the coming storm.

Noah, still pumping the chef's chest, shook his head like he couldn't believe what was happening. "I don't understand. Why won't he wake up?"

And that's when Jaden lifted a finger and pointed it at Laila. "It was her. Laila's cookie killed Chef Remi."

DAY TWO

C IS FOR COOKIES . . .
AND CRIME

LAILA'S JOURNAL ENTRY

Let's get something straight: I didn't almost kill Chef Remi. If someone reads this notebook, they'll know that. I'll make sure they'll know that. So I won't write this for Lucy, I'll write this for me. Lucy is asleep on the other side of the room, but she's never felt so far away before. I want to wake her up and talk it out like we always do. But I can't tell her what I did in the walk-in. Or that what Jaden said was true. I did cheat. All she needs to know is that I grabbed the butter and ran out. That I took a few moments to calm myself and that was the end of it.

She doesn't need to know the rest.

Last year, before the whole dance date debacle, she and Peter agreed that they would meet their adviser together and discuss them being co-editors in chief for the school newspaper. But then Peter submitted his application behind her back before the meeting. When Lucy got there, their adviser had already announced Peter the editor. He cheated and she was so mad . . . but said nothing. She hates him for it, and if she knew what I had done . . . she'd hate me too.

So I stopped thinking about how Lucy would be disappointed in me and the guilt. Instead, I created a masterpiece.

When Chef Remi pointed out every fault with Jaden's macarons, I smiled, which made me loathe myself more. At that moment, I wanted to win about as much as I wanted Jaden to lose. Then it all happened quickly. The room was unhappily clapping for me after Chef Remi said the nicest things about my cookies. I was about to win day one. The Golden Cookie was one step closer to being mine.

And then . . . well, Chef Remi nearly died, and Jaden said it was me.

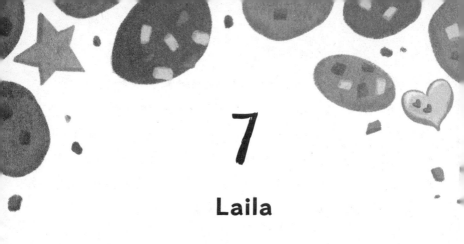

7

Laila

WHILE THE STORM was raging outside our dorm window last night, a storm raged in the pit of my stomach too. I pulled the notebook out of the pillow, finding the pen attached, and scribbled: *What was in Jaden's bag in the walk-in?* Which was when I noticed that my pen was a bit splotchy and I needed a new one.

I rolled off the bed and tiptoed over to the desk where Lucy's supplies were neatly organized. There were the dossiers on the competitors—more like folders with typed-up information—notebooks for each story she was working on, and somewhere there would be pens. Lucy never traveled without a backup case of pens.

I bent down and slipped my hand into her open backpack. Surely there were some in there? But I didn't find any. Instead, I pulled out another notebook. This one was smaller,

98

different in color from the others. It was one I hadn't seen before. I gently tugged at the flap, my eyes widening when I saw the heading.

"Laila Thomas: A Force with Flour"? It began by mentioning my life. My parents. My dad . . . his death. And then my cooking. I ripped through the pages, unable to focus on all the words. What was Lucy doing? What was this?

On the last page of her "notes," there were a few sentences underlined: *What is the connection between Laila and Chef Remi? What does it have to do with Jaden accusing her of cheating? Did she cheat?*

I pushed it back down, giving up the search for another pen, then bolted to the bathroom and heaved. Why would she think that about me? Why did she suspect *me*?

No, I told myself. No, I couldn't think about that. I wouldn't think about my best friend believing I had intentionally hurt Chef Remi. That I had anything to do with what happened. That she was writing some kind of exposé on me like her precious Ariella Wilborn.

The whole thing made my stomach gurgle again. Everyone treated me like I was the one who tried to kill Chef Remi. My friend was investigating when she should have left it to the professionals.

Or maybe I was sick because I hadn't eaten since the pizza yesterday.

Last night—before sending us to our rooms—they had given us dinner in the cafeteria, but no one had eaten. We barely spoke, except to the police detective who questioned us a little and the EMTs who checked on us and took Remi away, promising us they would do their best to save his life. Everything happened so fast because of the storm. Getting on campus was nearly impossible with the main road flooded and rolling power outages, so we barely had time to understand what had happened. Afterward, we called our parents on the landline before it got too unpredictable from the thunderstorm. Mom was still at her conference, so I was on my own anyway. Then the school administrators promised to set up a group Zoom in the morning with all the parents to discuss the future steps.

"Are you okay?" Lucy called through the door. Though her question was filled with concern, I heard the edge of distrust in her tone. She didn't know I found her little notebook or discovered she was trying to make a story out of me to get her scholarship.

The guilt and anger gnawed at the pit of my stomach, and I fought the urge to hurl again. My best friend thought the worst of me and there was nothing I could do. I took a few moments to breathe. The cool white tiles seeped through my pajama pants, and the fluorescent light made me squint.

"I'm okay," I responded carefully. I pulled myself off

the floor, nearly hitting the tiny shower stall before twisting around to the sink. Once I turned on the faucet, only the cold water worked, no matter how hot I tried to make it. With a sigh, I splashed my face with frigid water to wake up and be normal. To focus on the day ahead. Nothing else.

Dad's voice flitted into my head. *You're brave and talented, Laila, and there's nowhere you can't go. Nothing you can't do.* I repeated it a few times, but it didn't quite sink in. Not before the Zoom call anyway.

There was a pounding somewhere and a voice—Noah's voice—called out, "Kids, we have a meeting in ten minutes in the cafeteria! Don't be late, please."

Right. Because we had to talk about what happened again and what we're going to do. They were going to tell us the competition was over. The storm outside had caused flooding, cutting us off from the rest of the world, so we'd just have to sit there, waiting for the roads to be safe. And I didn't think my best friend was my best friend anymore.

All my dreams would fizzle into nothing. All because my cookies were the last Chef Remi ate. . . .

Lucy darted into the bathroom the moment I left it, and we finished getting dressed in silence. We brought matching shirts—neon pink, with chocolate doughnuts printed on them—to wear, but she chose a plain black tee. She might've forgotten, and I didn't want to remind her. We needed a break from each other. Until she told me why she was taking all those detailed notes about me, why she suspected me, I didn't want to be around her.

We left our dorm at the same time. She was chewing her bottom lip, clutching her backpack strap tight.

Philippa and Maeve fell in behind us, chatting about what'd happen.

"I bet they're going to stop the competition and send us all home once the roads clear," Maeve said with a sigh.

"If they do that, then I'll have my parents call and make sure we're offered spots in Sunderland in the fall. It wouldn't be fair if some guy nearly croaks and we all lose our chance to go here." Philippa's voice became a bit hysterical and loud. "I mean, if it wasn't . . . you know . . ." She trailed off, yet we all knew exactly what she was saying.

My shoulders sank, and I wanted to run away. I didn't hurt anyone, but everyone saw Chef Remi choke on *my* cookies. The truth would come out. It had to. The detective would tell everyone it wasn't me, and no one could argue with the professionals. Still, it seemed like no matter where I went and how well I did, people—even my best friend— wanted to believe the worst of me.

I swiped away a tear before Lucy saw it. She kept tossing me glances. She must've been wondering if I was a murderous monster all because I was so ambitious and I kept saying the wrong things. That's what her notebook implied. And the moment Lucy dug deeper and uncovered what I'd done . . . their labels and suspicions of me would be confirmed.

When we reached the cafeteria, Micah and Jaden were already there. They were sitting at different tables, both staring off at nothing. Maeve and Philippa grabbed a seat together while I went the opposite direction of Lucy. There was a big white screen set up in front of the empty cereal canisters and a laptop propped up on a stack of lunch trays. I was pretty certain that was where the Zoom call would take place.

Where my fate would be decided.

Maybe they were going to kick me out of the competition because of Jaden's accusations. Maybe the police checked into it, found some allergen or misused ingredient in the cookies, and they'd come back to arrest me in front of everyone. I knew it didn't matter if it was an accident, someone still almost died.

Mom was going to be so upset. She would have lost Dad and then me.

With that thought in mind, I plonked down at the table farthest from everyone and waited for the meeting. I had a bad feeling this wasn't going to go well. As if on cue, Philippa and Maeve began whispering about how my own best friend wasn't sitting by me. I couldn't hear them clearly, but I knew what they were saying: *Even Lucy doesn't believe her.*

Chef Polly strode in wearing a pastel-pink kaftan, holding a massive strawberry cake to match. She set it down on the table and produced a knife she must've had on her somewhere. She looked up at us as she expertly cut into the pink frosting.

"With the roads underwater, I realized we had nothing to eat but what was in our little ole kitchen," she said cheerfully, as if Chef Remi weren't in a hospital fighting for his life. Or maybe she was so cheery because he was. "Come on now, take a slice, don't be shy. This was my mama's recipe. Makes everyone feel a whole lot better, guaranteed."

No one jumped up to take the slice, and Chef Polly's face fell. "Now I know you all have gone through a terrible experience, but I've been assured—"

"That Chef Remi is alive in a coma." Noah walked in wearing a strangely colorful Hawaiian shirt and a big smile stretching his cheeks. "It's likely related to his heart issue, which he has had for over a decade. You wouldn't know it, but he'd been very unwell recently, and it's a shame that you all had to be here when his heart gave out."

"No way. It's her fault." Jaden tutted, glowering at me. None of the other contestants, including Lucy, came to my defense.

"We don't know that, Jaden." Noah shook his head, and

an edge crept into his voice. "It was likely no one's fault. And I'd appreciate you treating your fellow contestants with respect." Noah cocked his eyebrow, which seemed to close Jaden's mouth. "Now, come on, let's talk to your parents. They've been informed about what happened and many offered to come pick you up personally instead of sending your school vans. Laila, we haven't been able to reach your mother, I'm sorry to say. And Jaden, your father is out of state at the moment, but your papa will come get you on Sunday instead. Until then, they both said they know it's been hard and scary, but try to hang in there with your new friends."

We all turned to Jaden, whose cheeks turned a vibrant shade of red. He sputtered to himself. Normally, I might've found this funny, but I was too nervous I would be getting arrested for a crime I didn't commit.

Noah clicked on a few buttons from his laptop, and the white screen sprang to life. Squares featuring parents, administrators, and the detective we met yesterday popped up. Too many voices began speaking one over the other out of the laptop speakers. The connection wasn't good, and their faces would freeze on strange expressions, which gave me time to figure out who everyone was.

First, my mom wasn't there. Yes, Noah said she wouldn't be, yet part of me hoped she would show up anyway. But she was at the nurse conference and might not know about the whole incident that was going to ruin our lives. Second, both of Lucy's parents were there, sitting in their dining room with very solemn faces. I saw Lucy's junior journalism awards in the background. They hung on the worn lemon-print wallpaper next to the oversize wooden fork-and-spoon decoration they'd gotten from Lucy's grandma. Seeing it made my stomach settle a little. Only a little.

In the top left corner, with the crispest connection and in various shades of beige, were Philippa's parents. They were both striking blonds, and you could tell that Philippa was their pride and joy, since behind them were fancy portraits of her smiling in ball gowns and on horseback. They were already shouting.

"It's clear this competition is unsafe for our Philippa! Why haven't you arrested the girl who did it?" the mom shrieked. I could practically feel her gaze target me through the camera. "We don't want our daughter in the same place as a . . . as a murderer!"

"Mrs. Willingsworth, as I reminded you on our call last night, while we cannot rule out foul play, we are not arresting *any* contestant at this juncture," said the detective—a Black man with a dark gray suit and a very annoyed expression—in the bottom left of the Zoom screen. I think his name was Detective Valdez. "I reiterated this with every parent I spoke to in an attempt to not upset the children. Please don't make me remind you again. As of right now, this could very well be a simple accidental medical reaction—nothing has been eliminated as a possibility. We will need to investigate everything Chef Remi did and ate, and we will be looking into every contestant's background—"

"But why?" This time it wasn't the Willingsworths but a man who looked an awful lot like Micah, only much older. He was in a small gray room, possibly a storage shed. "What is there to investigate with our child? It's that girl who fed the chef poisoned—"

"There's no conclusive evidence of poison yet, Mr. Dae. The hospital stated as such, which I'm reiterating . . . again." The detective looked about ready to hang up and never deal with any of us.

I could barely feel relief at the detective's assurances when everyone was so adamant about blaming me. I was an outsider, a nobody from nowhere with nothing, who was the villain to their child's hero. I fought the urge to respond. Waiting and listening was the best way to not bring any more attention to myself—a lesson Lucy clearly didn't learn.

The detective continued. "In order to help Chef Remi recover, we will need lists of every ingredient in every cookie he ate. Along with—"

"I don't think that's necessary. We know that Remi got sick after eating that Laila girl's cookies, not Maeve's. I don't see why *my* child should be treated like a suspect." This time we all glanced up in the right corner, where the Issawis were sitting in a fancy black room—probably the office at one of their restaurants, judging by the "Best New Restaurant" newspaper clippings on the back wall. "We weren't watching the live stream, but I can assure you that Maeve would never do such a thing."

At that, a few parents mumbled about not being able to connect to the live stream either before Noah cut in.

"We are dealing with a storm. I promise you, we will sort the live stream issues and keep you posted. Now, to get back on the subject, we don't know what could have caused Remi's reaction or how long it could've taken to get into his system," Noah said authoritatively. "It could have been anything. Let's leave the speculation for the professionals."

It could have been anything? That meant it could have been in *any* of the cookies Chef Remi ate. . . . I could feel Lucy staring at me, but I didn't want to make eye contact. I couldn't believe she was focusing her scholarship story on my downfall. That was very unfriendly behavior for a friend.

"But, he was choking on *her* cookies!" Jaden shouted, pointing an angry finger at me. I knew he hated me, that he'd wanted me out before the competition began, yet it still hurt that anyone really thought I'd harm someone else. My stomach twisted. I wanted to respond, but my mouth was glued shut.

"Exactly!" Mrs. Issawi and Mr. Dae agreed at the same time. The other parents nodded along with them.

My back stiffened. It seemed like everyone wanted the attention on me. Wanted me to feel like a criminal, wanted me to be punished, and I couldn't understand why. Was it because of the way I looked? Because I came from a single-parent home? Because I didn't belong, didn't fit, didn't deserve to be in the same space as their precious kids? Why did everyone always treat me like I was someone bad? Why weren't my talent and compassion enough to be considered worthy like everyone else's? I was no different from the other contestants, yet unlike them, I couldn't be given the benefit of the doubt?

I looked up at Lucy's parents, silently begging them to stick up for me, but their screen was frozen and no one was coming to my defense. Even the detective was quiet.

"Heavens to Betsy!" Polly interjected with her strong southern accent. "I know Laila Thomas and I protest you talking about her that way. This girl is as innocent as a lamb, I'll tell you what! And y'all should be ashamed of yourselves. These children are traumatized when all they wanted to do was bake cookies. Now I know the Sunderland administrators are here on this call. Don't y'all have something to say?

Something that'll make these kids feel better?"

"Yes, we do," a stern woman with tan brown skin said. She was wearing a Sunderland lapel name tag that read "Principal Winters." "The doctors assured me on the phone that a cursory review of Remi's medical record supports that there's no certainty of foul play yet—he was incredibly ill—like the detective said. We know the police must investigate on the slim chance that this was intentional, though."

"That is correct," Detective Valdez cut in. "It's our job to make sure we've dotted all our *i*'s and dashed all our *t*'s, not just for all of you but for Chef Remi's doctors too, who are trying to figure out what could've caused this."

"Wait, I thought you said he had a heart problem. The doctors really don't have anything that can help our—your investigation?" Lucy asked, pen poised over her notebook, and I couldn't help but flash her a look of annoyance. She had to know every little detail, didn't she? For what, her article?

"They're running tests now, but don't worry: they're taking good care of him." The principal met Lucy's gaze. "Unfortunately, Chef Remi won't be back in this or any other kitchen anytime soon. It's so unfortunate you had to witness it. In the meantime, it's our recommendation that the competition go on as planned for those who are up for participating. Our school psychologist agrees that this would be the best way to work through the trauma and feel normal again. However, if any of you wish to opt out, we understand. It's your choice, we only want what's best for everyone."

We all ignored the idea of opting out, though I couldn't ignore what the school and detective said. "So, then you all know I didn't do anything to Chef Remi, right? You believe me?" I sat up in my seat, glancing at Lucy before settling on Noah. "That it wasn't my cookies? You're still letting me compete?"

"We will need a sample of each contestant's cookies and a detailed list of every ingredient everyone used. We'll also need to know exactly where each competitor was in the moments leading up to Chef Remi's episode," Detective Valdez said. "But we have no reason to doubt any of you . . . yet."

"Oh, Laila," Chef Polly said, holding a hand on her heart. "I'm sure your cookies had nothing to do with it, sweetie. Nothing to do with it at all. It was a tragic event, but no one could have done anything differently." She smiled again, and I found it weird because Chef Remi was in the hospital, not okay. She must really hate him. Or really believe in me.

"We're of course being ultracautious," Principal Winters said. "We're cooperating fully. This investigation is far from over. Polly was good enough to explain to us what happened when we weren't sure what to do. It could've been anyone's cookies, Laila, or anything. Polly and we at Sunderland agree that you should be able to compete. As far as we are concerned, not a single contestant is more innocent or guilty than anyone else."

A lot of parents began yelling again about how unfair it was that I was still there. I couldn't make out much of what they were saying other than how their child deserved a spot at the school more than me. That I didn't belong there to begin with. They were yelling so hard, they all got frozen like Lucy's parents. Noah didn't wait for the connection to be found again and closed the laptop, letting out a stream of air as if he were relieved.

"Looks like the storm picked up again," Polly said with a glance out the window. "But everything's been as resolved as it can be for the moment anyway." She began cutting the cake again, as if everyone would suddenly have their appetite back.

"I know this has been a lot, and as you may have guessed, you're still here partly because the storm has blocked off all roads. It's wreaking havoc on reception too. So you couldn't go home anyway, but I don't think you'll want to now that the competition is moving forward." Noah beamed at us from across the room. "I will be stepping in as a judge and taking on all of Chef Remi's responsibilities while he recovers."

Chef Polly's charm bracelet jingled as she took a paper

plate of cake and slid a fork onto it. "You can call your parents anytime. Although we have to remind everyone, there's only one working landline at the moment, so we may need to schedule it."

Noah began speaking too, but I zoned it out. I was too shaken up to think about eating. I didn't nearly kill Chef Remi. My cookies were fine and the police would figure that out. I was sure the samples would exonerate me.

Lucy had to believe me then, right? She'd drop it and apologize, throw away her terrible notebook, and we could go back to normal. The weight of the world seemed to lift off my shoulders and I suddenly did want a slice of that delicious-looking strawberry confection.

Then it sank in. We could compete again. It wasn't over yet; there was a chance for me to win and get into Sunderland with a scholarship. And though I was still very angry with Lucy, I knew we'd be okay eventually.

As everyone agreed to continue the competition, Chef Polly gave each of us a plate of cake. She told us to eat up and meet her in the kitchen arena in twenty minutes. Once she and Noah left—arm in arm, I might add—everyone seemed to let out a breath we didn't know we'd been holding in.

Lucy sat down at the table, next to me. I offered a small, warm smile in anticipation of her trying to console me, telling me that she saw the pressure I was under, that whatever secret notebook she had was a mistake and she didn't actually question my innocence.

Instead she leaned in and her voice was a dark whisper. "They're lying. Didn't you see how twitchy that detective was? He kept repeating the same lines over and over, like he had a script and was trying not to say something explosive."

"Can you drop it already?" I snapped, more than ready to move to a conversation that didn't revolve around me possibly being a criminal.

But she didn't seem to hear me or see how upset I was. "I think someone tried to murder Chef Remi. That's why the detective needs a list of everything in the cookies, why the doctors can't figure out what caused the reaction. It had to be something poisonous to Chef Remi, but fine for everyone else, and I'm going to prove it."

Anger tensed through my body and the fork fell from my hand. "Are you accusing me again like you did in your secret notebook about me? I told you—"

"Secret notebook? What are you . . ." Lucy shook her head, her brow furrowing briefly before she waved it off as if it didn't matter. "No, that's—that's not what you think. I can explain that and I know it looks bad, but you know me. Everyone was acting strange and we *need* to focus on that. Something happened to Chef Remi. If you want to clear your name, we should—"

I got up and gave her the angriest look I could muster as guilt spiraled in my gut. She wouldn't let this go. "You can't stop yourself, can you? I didn't do it, you know that. You're acting like all their mean parents." I waved around the room, drawing their renewed attention. "They all think I did it or I was involved, and you do too. You, who knows me best of all."

Lucy moved back, her lips drawn in a frown while her hands shot up as if to tell me to calm down. "I understand you're upset, but we need to get to the bottom of this. Then I can write about it for my scholarship piece!"

My breath caught in my chest, and angry acid climbed my throat. I couldn't believe she was going to pursue this. It wasn't lost on me that I was the one who encouraged Lucy to be all Ariella Wilborn in the first place . . . but not against *me*. She was supposed to be my best friend, supposed to support and believe me. If she dug around suggesting murder, they'd all say it was me again. They wanted it to be me so bad, they'd get a little nugget of my wrongdoing and do anything to prove I did worse things. People like me with brown skin and one parent who's always working but still not covering the rent were always the first to be blamed. Why couldn't she see that?

Lucy gripped her nonsecret notebook, and for the first time in our entire friendship, she looked confused. Her frown was more pronounced, her brow more furrowed, as if I'd puzzled her and she was suddenly unsure of me. Unsure how to respond to me. "I know this is a lot, and I hate that they threw your name around like that during the call. It might've seemed like everyone was against you, but not me. I'm just saying there's gotta be something more to what happened to Chef Remi, and anyone here could be responsible."

The room fell quiet, and everyone stared as my voice grew louder. "Stay away from me, Lucy, and if any of you still think I'm responsible, you can stay away from me too."

I left the cake on the plate and stalked out.

LUCY'S JOURNAL ENTRY

It's not like my best friend to leave cake uneaten.
Especially cake whipped up specially for us by a world-
renowned baker.

That's how I know Laila is this upset.

I'd tried to follow her to explain and smooth things
over. The thought of her being angry at me makes me
nauseous, like I was on a boat that suddenly barreled
down some rapids. From how wide her eyes got when
I mentioned my scholarship piece, I realized too late
that I'd said the wrong thing. But there were so many
questions and details speeding through my mind that
the words came out a mess. I thought it was clear I'm
investigating so I could clear her name, but I don't know
if she truly heard me. I don't blame her. She must feel
terrible after how awful everyone on that call was to

her. The glare she cast at me as she left the cafeteria made it clear: she wanted to be left alone right now.

Pressuring her to open up while she was trying to sort out her thoughts? That was a recipe for a disaster. Just like when I tried to get her to talk to me right after class about a science pop quiz she failed. She accused me of hassling her and she didn't speak to me the rest of that school day. But then she rage-baked some muffins at home and we talked it all out the next morning.

So I plopped back into my seat, pulled out this notebook, and tried to ignore the guilt tossing and turning in my stomach. I made my best friend feel worse. If only I had finished that profile piece on her by now: I could've surprised her with pages and pages of how wonderful and not criminal she is.

When Laila is finally ready to talk, I'll be there for her, like I always am. Until then, I'm going to have to do everything I can to clear her name, starting with noting how weird everyone else was acting during the big Zoom call this morning. Ariella Wilborn, investigative journalist extraordinaire, would tell me that even though I know Laila is innocent, I have to remain objective and put my feelings aside to chase every lead. So that's what I'll do. Laila will thank me when I get everyone to stop suspecting her.

An added bonus to helping my best friend—and not the main reason, which my garbage pile of words earlier might've made it seem—would be that my writing sample piece would jump from competition coverage to attempted murder investigation. Now that would blow the scholarship committee and Tonya away with the force of a hurricane for sure. All this would lead to Laila and me coming to Sunderland together for high school, like we planned.

The detective on the Zoom call wouldn't admit it to the parents, but I know what I heard when those other officers assumed I wasn't listening: this was foul play. Plus the deadly looks everyone cast at Chef Remi when they thought I wasn't looking? And how everyone's behavior was just a teensy bit off-kilter during the morning call? There's more to this than meets the eye.

And I'm going to be the one to blast this story wide open.

Then with a piece this strong? That Sunderland scholarship, Laila's good name restored, and four more years of best friendship would be guaranteed.

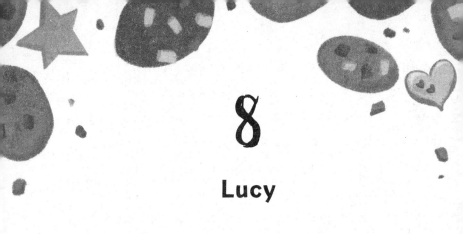

8

Lucy

I JOTTED DOWN my latest round of notes in my notebook to keep busy so I didn't chase after Laila and make things worse. I could at least kick-start my investigation by surveying the other competitors. I took another bite of Chef Polly's phenomenal cake. If we were going to be holed up on the Sunderland campus in the middle of a raging storm, with a wannabe murderer in our midst, at least we had good cake.

Even a minute of watching the others confirmed my conclusion earlier: everyone was acting oddly. Despite how critical she was of yesterday's pizza, Philippa was chasing her cake with glass after glass of the school's off-brand, watery orange juice without a word. Millionaire princess Philippa guzzling cheap drinks? Then across the table from her, Maeve sniffed her cake before taking a timid bite, like she was analyzing it. She leaned over to whisper something to Philippa, and the girls' eyes darted around the room like they were making sure they weren't being overheard.

Micah, who was so fitness focused he actually did push-ups at his workstation, approached Chef Polly for a third slice. My mom labeled herself an emotional eater, someone who tended to overindulge as a way of soothing her negative emotions. Maybe Micah was the same way. Guilt over attempted murder was probably a rather negative emotion. And Jaden . . . well, when wasn't he acting weird? He was waving his cell phone back and forth by the rain-pelted window, trying and failing to get a cell phone signal. He seemed almost frantic to reach someone outside of this place. Was that fear of getting hurt? Or fear of getting caught?

Granted, some of this behavior was to be expected: a man nearly died right in front of us less than twenty-four hours ago. The parents were up in arms about it, but the competitors seemed more relieved than upset that the competition was continuing.

That wasn't *expected*; that was *suspicious*.

No one even touched the stack of freshly printed quarter-page flyers Noah plopped on the table by the door. They were for an on-call grief counselor Sunderland hired. I didn't know how we were supposed to call them when we were stuck in the kitchen arena all day and on a limited landline schedule the rest of the time.

Jaden caught me eyeing him and his cell phone. "What are you looking at, Lucy? Shouldn't you be off with your bestie?" He smirked then. His face seemed a little pale. Anyone else would've chalked it up to the spotty light from the flickering overhead bulbs, but I noticed the shake in his smirk. He was using his bad attitude as a mask for something else: fear? "Oh, or did you realize I'm right? That Laila's the one who tried to kill the chef."

"You don't know that." It was a reflex for me to defend Laila, journalistic objectivity or not.

He shrugged. "Once this storm blows over and the roads clear, the cops will show up again and arrest her. You'd better get your own story straight or they'll handcuff you too."

I scowled. "You think I had anything to do with this?"

"You're stuck to Laila like glue. I don't know why you're here!"

I tightened my grip on my fork. "I told you, I'm covering this for our school paper."

"Oh yeah?" Lightning flashed, and Jaden's gaze flitted over to the backpack hanging from my chair. A corner of my notebook peeked out. "Then prove it. Show us what you've been writing in there. I think Laila is cheating—it wouldn't be the first time—and you're helping her somehow."

My stomach twisted. Laila and I included every tiny detail in our notebooks last night, including our not-so-nice judgments about the other competitors. I didn't like Jaden at all, but I still hated the thought of having him angry at me. I couldn't show *anyone* our private notes.

Right about now was when Laila would've come to my defense, if she were here. She would've told Jaden to mind his own business, that people are innocent until proven guilty.

"You're way off base. Just leave us alone, Jaden." I was here to investigate and clear my friend's name, not to argue with jerks like him. There wasn't anything I was going to learn from Jaden being rude to me. I grabbed my backpack and cake and walked out of the cafeteria. After dropping into one of the tacky orange lounge chairs nearby, I finished my slice in peace and added this morning's observations to my notebook. I considered calling my parents, but my phone didn't have a single service bar. Getting good cell reception here was like playing Whac-A-Mole at an arcade: it would be complete chance if you happened to be standing in the right spot, at the right time, to be blessed with a bar or two. I headed to the kitchen arena as the other competitors started to make their way there too.

Laila was standing at a different workstation by the time I walked in behind Micah. They must have let her switch because, well, it was creepy—and distracting—to be a foot away from where someone almost died with your cookie in their mouth.

I went straight for my empty workstation to sit by myself. Noah joined Chef Polly at the judges' table. The kitchen stayed eerily quiet as the competitors tied on their aprons and washed up. I set my notebook and favorite pen in front of me, and it was actually comforting having these at hand. They were like a sword and shield.

And figuring out who wanted to murder Chef Remi was the epic battle I was about to launch myself headfirst into.

Chef Polly rounded the judges' table and clapped to get everyone's attention. Not like she needed to make that much noise in such a silent room. "We were going to do a technical challenge, but since there wasn't a winner yesterday, it's the right time to shake things up. Noah and I decided that this morning's challenge seems particularly apt. Our theme is distraction. They say distraction can help cope with difficult emotions."

Everyone's eyes drifted to the spot where we last saw Chef Remi. A chill ran down my spine. Some of the competitors didn't even blink. Philippa actually looked annoyed. I'm sure it's annoying when you keep getting reminded of how you hurt someone, though. I jotted that down.

Chef Polly clasped her hands together tightly. The move struck me as odd: she was such an animated talker, her hands waving as she spoke on her TV show or earlier to the competitors. But now, it was like she didn't know what to do with them. "I'm sure y'all know how hard it is to concentrate on assigned reading or decade-old documentaries. So show us, using your cookies, what you'd rather be doing."

"And before you ask," Noah cut in, "no, you can't bake a scene of you baking cookies!"

Then everyone laughed.

Laughed, in a room where someone almost died yesterday.

Even Laila.

What was going on? I paused my writing. How would I narrow down suspects when everyone was acting suspiciously?

Noah started the countdown clock, and it was only then that the kitchen returned to its normal bustle. Feet shuffling, metal bowls clanging, mixer engines humming.

For my school paper piece, I scrawled down details about the competitors, this latest challenge, what it looked like everyone was making. That took only ten minutes, so I started to flip back through the notes Laila and I wrote together. Then I read through them again.

There was nothing out of the ordinary leading up to the end of the second round. It was summer, so the Sunderland campus was empty. Golden Cookie judges Chef Remi and Chef Polly and administrator-turned-judge Noah got here first. Then all the competitors arrived. Our rooms were right next to each other, and everyone was either stuck in the kitchen arena or in the cafeteria together at the same time. That made it really tricky for someone to do some dastardly ingredient switch.

Philippa *did* bring her own marble-handled knife, despite competitors being told not to bring outside tools. My heart warmed thinking about Laila's reaction when she read my note about Philippa's fancy personalized knife.

Last night, I'd expected Laila to growl about Philippa's rule breaking. I didn't expect her to start laughing so hard that she stopped breathing. Of course I joined in, though I wasn't quite sure what we were laughing at.

Once she calmed down, Laila shook her head. "The things rich folks spend their money on."

I raised an eyebrow. "You're right: she's rich. She doesn't need the full-ride scholarship you're all competing for. We need to find out why she's here."

"Maybe she just wants to show off her lucky, personalized, marble-handled knife to a new audience," Laila said, wiping a laugh-induced tear away from her eye.

After the long, stressful day one we'd had, it had been nice to have a brief moment of joy with my best friend, before it all went sour when her story didn't add up.

I hated having Laila angry at me. I stumbled over my words in urging her to help me investigate, and I still hadn't gotten a chance to work things out with her. But at the root of it, I was doing this not only for the scholarship writing sample but to get rid of all that suspicion around my best friend. I didn't mean to hurt her, and I'll show how sorry I am by continuing to cheer her on and, of course, finding out who really hurt Chef Remi.

I plucked a highlighter out of my backpack and drew a box around the notes about Philippa's knife. This changed things. This meant that at least one of the competitors was a rule breaker. So who else might've snuck something into Sunderland that they weren't supposed to?

Micah had a plant, didn't he? I wondered what the rules on that were.

Ahead, Noah strolled from workstation to workstation, as Chef Remi did yesterday. Though instead of sarcastic comments, he doled out smiles and encouraging words. Maeve actually blushed when Noah paused by her and took a sincere interest in her work.

Noah eyed the beginnings of a helix Maeve was crafting from black-and-white cookies. "DNA? Marvelous."

"I'm cocaptain of our science decathlon team," she squeaked.

Noah's laugh was warm, like when an uncle pretended to be wowed by how tall you've grown. "And you're a talented baker? You're full of surprises, Maeve."

"Thank you, Chef." Maeve blushed further before laser

focusing back on her work. It was like she didn't want the attention, which was odd for a competition based on making your baking stand out.

I flashed back to the Zoom we had with everyone's parents. The Issawis had proudly displayed articles about their daughter's science decathlon wins on the walls behind them. So how much did Maeve know about chemicals and reactions? And was it enough to be dangerous?

Noah headed to Laila's new workstation next. My shoulders tensed. I knew he was the furthest thing from Chef Remi and that Laila was angry at me, but I still didn't want anyone to say a single bad thing about her cookies. I had relatives who pocketed Laila's cookies in the middle of big family gatherings just so they could enjoy the sugary treats later too. Even Chef Remi seemed to come around to Laila's fabulous skills by the end of round two.

Whatever Noah whispered to her, Laila proudly responded with, "Thank you, Chef!"

I tried to catch her eye then, to send her a telepathic "Great job!" But she didn't look at me. It's like she was purposely trying to ignore me.

I had to admit, I was a little deflated. I was here not only for the school paper and writing samples but to support her as a friend. Why was she so bent on keeping me from investigating and doing what friends do—supporting each other?

Maybe this had something to do with that gap of time she spent in the walk-in yesterday. The gap she refused to tell me more about.

This was the girl who shared every uncensored thought about Micah the Mighty and his biceps. The fact that she was obviously keeping something from me—and for this long—was a huge deal. We were supposed to be best friends. She was supposed to be able to share everything with me, especially an alibi for a crime she'd been accused of. I was giving her space, but at some point, I would've liked some answers too. Not only for my investigative piece, but as a friend being ignored.

Then Laila's words from earlier came back to me so fast they almost knocked me off my stool: she had mentioned the secret notebook.

I had been so determined to kick off the investigation that I'd missed what she said. This meant she must have found the notes I was keeping for the town paper profile. And as I stared down at my suspect list now, my notes looked incredibly similar to that profile prep in my other notebook, down to the stars I drew next to points I considered important.

She must have thought I considered her a suspect. Maybe *the* suspect. Oh no. All the background on her was just for the town paper profile. And the recent notes? That was just me getting the timeline straight—exactly who was where, and why, throughout the competition. It wasn't geared toward her specifically, but she might not have understood that. It was like how my bedroom looked like a pigsty to my mom but I knew precisely where everything was. I had a system, a whole thought process that other people didn't understand. I had to clear this up with Laila the second this round was over.

"One more hour, competitors!" Chef Polly announced from the judges' table. She glanced down at her phone and pursed her lips. She wasn't getting reliable cell phone service either, then, like Jaden and me. This storm must've knocked out a cell tower nearby.

A crack of thunder shook the windows, like the storm was admitting its guilt.

With Laila and the rest of the competitors lost in their work, I decided to get some action shots for the paper. I carefully pulled the school DSLR camera out of my backpack. From my seat, to avoid disrupting the competitors, I snapped some photos of Maeve precisely measuring cup after cup of sugar. Micah used a wooden spoon to manually mix his batter, his biceps flexing with each turn. Philippa beamed up at Noah, who was pointing at something on her workstation (her personalized knife, maybe?). Laila's eyebrows scrunched up with extreme concentration as she added food coloring to her icing drop by drop. I purposely chose angles that didn't have Jaden in them.

As I reviewed the shots, I caught a glimpse of something behind Chef Polly at the judges' table.

A webcam.

That must be for the live stream.

I spun around on my stool to find the camera near me. When Noah showed me to this empty workstation yesterday, he had asked me to watch where I placed myself so I didn't block people's views. I suddenly remembered a few parents complaining about the spotty live stream connection, but maybe someone out there saw something that would prove Chef Remi was being targeted!

My heart hammering in my chest, I scanned the wall of shelves behind me. Then I saw it: a sleek black webcam, nestled between shiny box graters. My dad had this same expensive webcam for his gaming live streams. From here, viewers would've been able to see the full kitchen arena in crystal-clear detail.

But then my heart thudded to a stop. The indicator light was dark. It was supposed to be a bright red, which was how I knew whether I could ask Dad something without his Twitch followers hearing me. Over a hundred people witnessed me telling him my "tummy felt ickypoo" after gas station sushi last month.

I whirled around and squinted to spot the webcam

behind Chef Polly. That indicator light was dark too. And so was the one on the webcam positioned by the door.

I photographed the three webcams with the DSLR camera, for evidence.

The high-definition webcams that were supposed to broadcast every juicy moment of the prestigious Golden Cookie Competition to the world?

Someone had switched them all off.

LAILA'S JOURNAL ENTRY

I'm the first one in the kitchen, so I take out my notebook and start writing down every ingredient that I used in my cookies like the detective asked. I meant to do it last night, but with everything going on and the fight, I couldn't focus. Then I place that paper on the table for Noah and retrace my steps. I stand in the walk-in, remembering what I did there. Searching for traces.

On one of the shelves where Jaden kept his macarons, there's still some of the brown powder that I'd seen from his baggie. There's only one—*slightly dangerous*—way to figure out what it is. And anyway, danger is better than being accused of murder, which is what'll happen if Lucy and all the competitors and parents have their way. So I lick my finger and touch the powder. Bring it to my lips and taste. . . . It has an earthy flavor. Not hazelnut flour like I thought, rather like leaves. Fragrant leaves. Like tea, maybe? Chamomile tea, to be exact. Why would Jaden have a baggie full of tea in the walk-in? It doesn't make much sense. There must have been something else, some other reason he was in there so long.

Although there's a chance I'm wrong.

Yet I can't look around further, and I need to tuck this journal away and focus on baking. I have to get back to the kitchen and be ready for the next round. And I can't afford to lose.

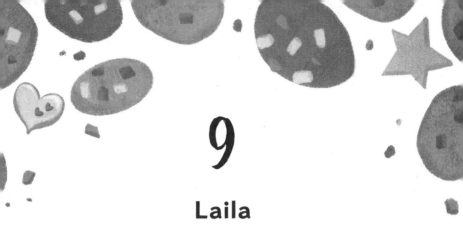

9

Laila

NOTHING WAS WORKING out and I didn't feel brave or talented.

I'd already burned two batches of cookies, and while my icings were colorful perfection, that wouldn't matter if I had nothing to ice.

Everyone else was doing amazing, as if that call with their parents and their support (and throwing me under the bus) gave them strength. Jaden was making a three-dimensional cookie of a camera, Micah was making his family's greenhouse, Maeve was making a DNA helix, Philippa was making a horse, and I . . . I realized I had nothing and no one else right now other than Lucy. So I was crafting Lucy out of cookies and I kept burning her or creating crumbly, inedible dough. Because whenever we fought, I was a mess.

An angry, lonely mess.

Jaden knocked my shoulder as he stalked by and snickered at my attempt at slicing cookie dough into the shape of Lucy's face. "Nerves getting to you? Worried about how you'll look in an orange jumpsuit?" Tears filled my eyes and he sneered. "The moment I get some decent cell reception, I'm going to tell everyone it's your fault Chef Remi's in the hospital. You won't get into Sunderland, you won't get into college. People will always know you as the girl who tried to kill a culinary legend." And with that, he sauntered off.

My hands slammed down on the table. I didn't try to kill anyone, and yet I'd lost my best friend, and everyone hated me or believed I had done something bad. With a flick of my wrist, I tossed another batch of cookie dough into the trash. There was a little less than one hour left, and there was only one dough that'd work at this point. My cream cheese sugar cookies. Soft, fluffy, took shape well. Right, back to the walk-in. The walk-in where all my troubles started.

I bolted past Philippa and Maeve, who were assembling their architectural masterpieces. There was no time for me to do that. I was going to have to keep it flat, which'd definitely prevent me from placing first.

Micah gave me a smile as I passed by, and I wished I could smile back, yet my face wouldn't let me. I was determined, and the tears dangled precariously from my eyes, waiting for the moment to break free and embarrass me.

I darted into the walk-in and gave myself a moment to breathe. *Breathe in, breathe out, breathe.*

Lucy and I agreed to never be what people expected of us. We'd be the best versions of ourselves whenever we could: an agreement we made after Peter cheated her out of the co-editor in chief position. So me doing what I did in the walk-in would make her think less of me. That wasn't honorable: that's what people expected of a single-mom-raised kid from the bad side of town.

Somehow, the idea of Lucy thinking so poorly of me that she'd keep a hidden notebook and question my role in Chef Remi's near demise made the tears break free and stream down my face. The air was already cold, and my tears felt like they were freezing. Instead of pushing the feelings aside, I let them be.

A sob clawed its way out of my throat, and I leaned against a rack holding all kinds of fruits and doughs and vegetables. Things shook on the shelves and something fell somewhere, and before I knew it, the door swung open and weirdly strong arms wrapped around me.

"There, there, honey," whispered Chef Polly. "It's okay." Though she was small and like a million years old, she held me tight and let me cry a bit. "I know this is so tough. But you're doing great. You all are."

I whimpered something that didn't happen to be words.

"You don't blame yourself, do you? Oh, those mean parents on that call. Ignore them. It wasn't you or your cookies." Chef Polly rubbed my back in circles, and I inhaled the scent of strawberry cake on her and some floral perfume I couldn't place.

"How can you be so sure?" I asked through the tears. I expected her to say the same thing she'd said earlier, about how it was his faulty heart and how the doctor agreed. Instead she surprised me.

"I know these things. Chef Remi often worked himself up with all that negativity. He'd get so mad and . . . and . . . nonsensical. It's a wonder that man has lived as long as he has with that bad outlook on life, not to mention how many people hated him. He shut down mom-and-pop restaurants, he bankrupted good working people, took away jobs from people who well and truly deserved them, and he treated everyone who worked with him and for him like inferiors. I can't imagine how relieved poor Noah is to have a break." She was talking faster than I'd ever heard her. Her southern accent slipped a little and sounded harder, less lyrical. "No, it wasn't you, honey. Don't worry: Chef Remi's in the hospital and the best medical teams are going to try to get him back on his feet. But I assure you, the culinary world would be a better place with him not in it."

And that was when I started suspecting that Chef Polly

wasn't really speaking to me at all. It seemed as if she were talking to herself. Telling herself these very same words, as if she were also upset . . . or she was guilty of something too.

When I moved a little away and looked up at her, she was back to smiling again. "Don't you waste another tear on that man. Yesterday, you were on track to win; now it seems like you're falling behind. Get back out there and show us what you got, okay?"

I sniffed and nodded a few times, glancing away. Partially hidden among the stacks of butter, there was a small white-and-orange bottle. It looked like a prescription bottle, like the ones my dad had needed toward the end of his illness. I couldn't make out the lettering on it. Why would medicine be in the walk-in? Odd.

"Good. I'm rooting for you," Polly said, bringing my attention back to her. "Shall we?"

She waited until I grabbed my cream cheese and left with her, although I desperately wanted to swipe that bottle and inspect it further.

Lucy was so certain it was foul play. Was there really a potential murderer in our midst—one who might not be exposed if we didn't step in and bust the case ourselves? Were we in danger? What if sweet Chef Polly was the one who tried to kill him? Or maybe Noah did. Maybe there was something to Lucy's murder theory.

Still, I had to compete, and it wasn't the time to go over to Lucy and tell her everything. I was already behind schedule. Winning wasn't an option at this point, yet failing wasn't either. I had to put in enough effort to show that I could pull off a win.

So I got back to my station and whizzed through the cookies, a new resolve washing over me. I'd tell Lucy everything, even if it made her disappointed in me. And then *she'd* tell me why she was writing about me. We would clear this all up, apologize, and be friends again. I hoped. Because if there was foul play involved, it wasn't safe for any of us to be alone.

I took my gigantic flat cookie from the oven. It was the shape of Lucy's face and hair and holding a notebook. It wasn't really artistic. In fact, it looked a lot like a blob. And I had only thirty minutes to make it look like something else.

With my piping bags full of colored icings, I got to work, making Lucy's face and coloring her in. It was such a mess, and the clock was ticking loudly in my ears and my heart was racing and I was disappointed, so disappointed, but I had to keep going. When the time was called, everyone put their tools down and laughed and clapped. Except me.

Because mine looked like an explosion when it should've looked like Lucy.

Noah and Chef Polly started with Maeve's gingerbread

DNA helix. "Phenomenal construction and tasty!"

Then they stopped to judge Micah's greenhouse made from various types of teas and honey and spices. "This is the most adventurous we've seen you with flavors, Micah. It's still a tiny bit bland, but we can tell you put your heart and home into this rendition of your family's greenhouse with the execution."

Philippa beamed when the chefs stopped by her bench to critique her three-foot horse. "A horse made out of cookies! So innovative and creative!"

Jaden was next with his intricate camera made from raspberry linzer cookies that looked snappy and delicious. "Absolutely perfect!"

Noah went so far as to say Jaden was a true artist.

And then they stopped at mine, and their faces fell. "What happened?" Noah asked, eyeing my monstrosity of sugar cookies.

Chef Polly cut in. "Who is this supposed to be? A character from a favorite show?"

The shame burned brightly on my face, no doubt. "It's supposed to be Lucy." And at that, I finally glanced over at my former best friend I'd been ignoring for the past hours. She gave me a small smile. One that said she was waiting for me to open up to her and that nothing was as bad as it seemed. I really hoped that was possible. I wanted it to be possible.

"It's a shame, you were the top of the competition yesterday, but today you're the bottom. Do you think you'll do better in the next challenge?" Noah's voice carried a wave of sadness, while his facial expression seemed distracted at best. It seemed like stepping into Chef Remi's role meant being a little more critical and aloof too.

"Now wait a second, we haven't tasted it yet." Polly didn't give me a chance to sputter reasons why I should be there competing and why I did worse today than yesterday. But someone almost died. The police were investigating me. I could go to jail! And while the other contestants could move past it, it seemed I couldn't. Shouldn't I have gotten some credit or at least understanding for that? Polly grabbed a chunk of cookie and took a teeny, tiny bite. "It's incredible!"

Then Noah pursed his lips and reluctantly broke off a piece. With each chew, his smile grew. "The cookie base is probably one of the fluffiest, tastiest sugar cookies I've ever had. The icing also has a creaminess I wasn't expecting. I was wrong, but—"

"But in the next challenge, you're going to have to do better, right?" Chef Polly finished with a wink. I nodded a bunch till Noah walked off, while Polly remained. She leaned in close. "What we discussed in the walk-in, that's our little secret, okay?"

I nodded again. "Okay."

She grinned at me, and then she and Noah named Micah the Mighty the winner of the challenge, followed by Maeve, Jaden, Philippa, and me in last place. Unlike when I won yesterday's first challenge, the judges decided Micah would be given some sort of an advantage in the next round. I tried not to be jealous. Soon, everyone was chatting and Jaden kept glancing at my cookie and laughing.

I excused myself, although no one was looking at me anyway, and headed back to the walk-in. On bent knees, I yanked the pill bottle from under the rack. It was empty, and most of the label had been torn off, but the name on it was easy to read.

Jaden Parker.

I shoved it into my pocket and darted back to the kitchen arena, where everyone was sampling each other's cookie masterpieces, except mine. As I pretended to be happy for Micah, all I could think about was telling Lucy in private that I thought she was right to keep digging.

Someone in this competition did try to put murder on the menu after all. Possibly the one person who kept pointing his finger at me from the beginning.

10

Lucy

I STUFFED EVERYTHING into my backpack as quickly as I could. Even the DSLR camera. I winced, too late, when I heard it thunk against my notebook and pens. But I had to get to Laila to explain before she could storm off again.

I zipped up my backpack and lunged toward her workstation as everyone else exited the kitchen to head to lunch. The kitchen double doors swung shut. We were alone. Thunder rumbled somewhere in the distance.

"I'm sorry," we both said at the same time. Then we did this awkward snort-laugh at the same time too.

Laila began folding her polka-dot apron on the counter between us. She was wearing her neon-pink chocolate-doughnut shirt, and I was so in my head this morning that I'd forgotten about mine. She must have felt so alone after everything, and I felt awful that my behavior probably didn't help that.

Laila spoke first. "I'm sorry I didn't tell you what I was doing in the walk-in yesterday. I'm just . . . embarrassed by it. Jaden had pushed me and walked out." I gasped. I couldn't believe I ever doubted her when it was evil Jaden who was up to no good. "I was so mad about what he did and what he said," she continued, her brow furrowed. "The butter was gleaming at me from the shelf, and all I had to do was take it and go. But then he sorta shoved me and I gave him rancid almond flour, figuring he was making macarons, which was a serious miscalculation, because . . ." She paused her folding. "Chef Remi had a whole section of his latest cookbook dedicated to his grandma's macaron recipes and there was no way Jaden could compete. And with bad almond flour, they would taste terrible. Plus, I knew that if he was making macarons, he was going to come back for egg whites . . . so . . ."

"Laila, come on," I said with a small smile. I knew how she got when she talked about the love of her life, baking. We could be here for days and I needed to know, a little more quickly than that, what happened.

She scrunched her nose like she was offended. "Anyway. If I added a little egg yolk to the pasteurized egg whites, it would never whip up properly. He'd fail. So I . . . I did.

I took the egg white container and poured egg yolk in. I cheated because I cheated before. Jaden was right. I cheated the last time we met. I didn't mean to, but it happened and he wouldn't stop talking about it."

Air whooshed out between her teeth and I saw the cracks in her confidence. How did I not notice them before? Then she found all my town paper profile notes and assumed I turned on her too? Before I could apologize for not realizing how awful this all was for her, she threw her hands in the air.

"The apple pie competition. The judge knew me. She's friends with my parents—my mom. She knew how tough I was taking Dad's death . . . how baking was the thing we did together. She knew how bad I wanted to win and let me. And maybe that's not cheating, but if I were in Jaden's shoes, I'd think it was." She shook her head, her eyes misty. "And then Chef Noah said I wasn't supposed to be here. Like I didn't belong because of where we're from and our families. And I was so embarrassed because . . . it seems like people like me aren't supposed to win. We're bad. We're criminals. They expect the worst of us and then feel good when we prove them right."

I stared at her, then reached across the counter and placed a hand on her arm to let her know I was here and I cared.

She exhaled slowly, her fingers worrying the hem of her

apron. "I realized that I would hate myself for sabotaging Jaden . . . so when I walked by his bench, I swapped the egg whites with a fresh carton without him noticing. He was making mistake after mistake without me . . . still, I didn't touch the almond flour, though. He should've checked that himself, right?"

"Not everyone has your sense of supertaste," I cut in. "But you're right, that's on him to know what he's putting into his cookies. Second, anyone who thinks you don't belong here is a butt."

She nodded, encouraged by my small agreement and the use of the word *butt,* probably. "Anyway, no win is worth cheating again. What would my dad say? What would Mom say? What would *you* say?"

My stomach twisted throughout her confession. The Laila I knew wouldn't sabotage another competitor. But the pressure of this competition, all that's riding on it, and the way everyone immediately pointed fingers at her for what happened to Chef Remi: maybe it was taking more of a toll than she'd admit to me. Was I so focused on the almost murder and my article that I didn't see that? What kind of friend was I?

My silence must have made her nervous, because her next words came out rapid-fire.

"It's why I didn't say anything earlier. I didn't want you

hating me for being a bad person and I knew that if everyone found out what I'd done, they'd think I was capable of worse . . . but I definitely don't want you thinking I'm a murderer!"

Her volume rose at her last words, and a tear finally slipped out of her eye. I should've been more aware of how she was feeling, how shaky her confidence was. I was here to prove myself as an investigative journalist, but I had to prove I was a good friend first. We were stuck on campus with someone who tried to kill the chef. We needed each other; we always have.

I rounded the workstation to stand next to her. "First of all, I don't think I could ever hate you. I don't like that you were going to lower yourself to cheating, especially with as well as you've been doing. But you tried to fix it, and that says a lot about you. You had the opportunity to ruin Jaden, and you definitely had the motive: he's a real jerk."

Laila cracked a small smile.

"Also, you couldn't control what that judge did at the apple pie competition, and who's to say you didn't bake the best apple pie at the competition after all? Yours is pretty amazing. That crust? Whew. Anyway, I could see why the judge being your dad's friend would make you second-guess your skills, but you shouldn't. Apple pie competition win or not, Jaden shouldn't treat you as terribly as he does. I'm actually proud of you because you chose to be the better person."

She smudged away the tear with the back of her hand. "Really? Proud? Even after this?" She pointed at the cookie that looked like someone threw me in a blender.

We both laughed, and I already felt the tension between us crumbling away. It was a relief. I couldn't stand the thought of her being upset with me. "Laila, you're the most talented baker I know. I wish you'd believe that about yourself too. But, um, this cookie? Let's just say it's not your best work."

"I'm so embarrassed I put that in front of the judges. How could I let myself get thrown so off-balance? This will knock me out of the running for first place for sure. Then my baking career's over before it's begun."

"Hey, quit beating yourself up. I'm sure you'll bounce back. I can't believe anyone seriously thinks you would've hurt Chef Remi."

Laila's eyes widened then. "I mean, I *know* I didn't, but how'd you come to that conclusion after being so suspicious of everyone earlier? You even had all this info on me, like the dossiers you made on the other contestants."

My stomach sank. "So you did find my notes! I swear, it's not what you think!"

"Then what is it? Because it definitely looked like you

thought I could be guilty."

I shook my head. It wouldn't be the grand surprise I wanted, but I couldn't have my best friend thinking I didn't believe her. "Those notes about the competition were about everyone and everything, not just you, so I could sort it out and help clear your name. And the rest of it? I'm actually doing a profile on you for the town paper, something to highlight how amazing you are. That's why I was collecting all that info before. It wasn't because I thought you were a criminal: it's because I think you're the best."

Laila's shoulders eased down, like starting to clear up that misunderstanding was taking weight off of her. "I—um—thanks, Lucy."

"Well, don't thank me yet," I said. I rubbed the back of my neck. "I haven't written the profile. And now it won't be a surprise. All it did was make you think I didn't trust you."

"I have to admit that part of the reason I was so angry about you investigating is because I could tell you were poking around about me too. But I would've never guessed it's for some fancy profile." She smoothed the folded apron flat with her palm. "And you're right to keep looking into what happened to Chef Remi. I thought if I could just focus on the competition, it'd get me back on track to win, but I get the feeling there's even bigger stuff going on too."

I leaned in. "There is. Get this: I think someone turned

off the cameras that are supposed to be live streaming this event."

Laila gasped. "So no witnesses? But everyone's parents—"

I shook my head. "They couldn't watch. Remember how Maeve's parents mentioned something weird with their live stream? Everyone figured the storm was messing with the connection. But it's possible it was never working at all. For anyone."

"This camera stuff does feel big. And check out what I found in the walk-in."

From her pants pocket, Laila pulled out an empty pill bottle and tossed it to me. I caught it and read the label: *Jaden Parker.* "It was behind the butter, like he was trying to hide it," she said. "What kind of pills were in this bottle and how did they end up in the walk-in?"

I handed the bottle back to her. "I guess that's on my list of things to figure out. It's fishy for sure: Jaden was in and out of the walk-in before Chef Remi got poisoned."

Laila frowned. "The kid has secrets."

"And Philippa might too. That rich girl has definitely been acting like she's hiding something."

I yanked my notebook out of my backpack to write down our discussion. There were too many people involved, too many loose threads to untangle, too many things people wanted to keep hidden.

"If you've got a list of suspects," Laila said, watching me as I wrote, "maybe put Chef Polly on there. I love her, but when I was chatting with her earlier, she said some stuff that made her sound a little too glad to be rid of Remi. Maybe she could have shut off the cameras?"

I paused, considering. "She does have free rein around the school."

Laila tapped her fingers on the counter. "And during the competition, the judges walk around. I wouldn't have noticed what they were up to, and neither would the other competitors, if we were all laser focused on baking."

I thought then of Chef Polly frowning and mashing at the screen of her phone the way my grandma does. "Then again, Chef Polly doesn't seem too . . . tech savvy."

"For all we know, it could be an act. She's on TV all the time: she's probably used to showing herself a certain way. Like how all those super-nice charitable celebrities get outed for being total bullies. It might be worth looking into, but the next round is right after lunch. I can't compete and keep an eye on Chef Polly at the same time."

I put my hand on her shoulder. "You worry about baking your heart out. I'll investigate this camera stuff while you're winning round four. You'll just have to cover for me. Maybe say I'm not feeling well? That I have—"

"Explosive diarrhea!"

"—a headache." I twisted my face at her suggestion, and she laughed. "Ew, nothing digestion related or they'll never let me back into the kitchen. I'll see what I can find and slip back in to see you win the round."

"You sure you can do that? Noah is intense about competition rules, and after Chef Remi . . ."

"The rules say no one can leave the kitchen arena once the round starts. They don't say you can't come in late."

"And if the rest of us are stuck in the arena, it's not like someone can pop in and check on you and your alibi. Perfect. You'll have a whole two hours to check this out."

"Three, if I start now."

"But what about lunch?" As if on cue, Laila's stomach grumbled. That was on her for leaving Chef Polly's delicious strawberry cake behind this morning. "You have to eat something."

She reached past me to break a piece off the BlenderFace-Lucy cookie: the head, to be precise. Then she shoved it right in my face. "I know how you get when you're hangry. I'm not resting both our Sunderland admissions on your cranky, low-blood-sugar butt. Here."

"I'm not that bad, am I?"

Laila suppressed a smile. "You think Ariella Wilborn

would let herself run on fumes?"

"I had a slice of cake this morning! That should be enough."

Laila sighed. "Remember when you got hangry at your little brother's birthday party and shoved your cousin into the pool?"

Laila loved to remind me of this. My mom immediately forced a plate in my hand, then shooed me up to my room until I could calm down and my cousin could dry off. Meanwhile, Laila got to keep splashing outside but kept glancing around to see where I'd disappeared off to. I couldn't exactly open my window and yell to her without Mom catching me. The only way I could signal to her was by flicking the lights on and off, like using Morse code, which I didn't actually know. She saw me and thought it was hilarious.

"Fine." I took a bite of the cookie Laila offered and actually groaned aloud at how good it was. "Like I told you," I said as I broke off another piece of my cookie-self ear, "you're the best baker I know."

She beamed, like it was just what she needed to hear at that precise moment. While I chewed, she reached for the wooden knife block and pulled out a small, serrated knife. "If you're going to be wandering around this empty building all by yourself, take this."

I eyed the tiny blade. "What am I supposed to do with

this? Peel an apple to distract the murderer?"

Laila rolled her eyes. "First of all, this isn't even the right knife for that. This is a steak knife. And it's just to buy you some time if someone jumps out at you, I don't know. I just figured you didn't want to be roaming around with some big horror-movie meat cleaver. No offense, but you don't have the upper-body strength for that."

"Um, I'll pass on the knife. I'll take something for self-defense, though." I grabbed a sturdy-looking wooden spoon and slid it into the side pocket of my backpack, then reached for the BlenderFaceLucy cookie again. "You're right that we have to be more careful from now on. We don't know who tried to kill Chef Remi or if they've got anything out for the rest of us. How about you, though? Are you going to be all right in here, with everyone else?"

"I've got all these sharp objects at my disposal," she said, waving her arm out with a flourish, like a magician. "Plus, I can do some damage with a rolling pin, and everyone here knows it."

I nodded. Normally, in horror movies, the last thing anyone should do was go off alone. That was how someone ended up in some creaky attic or an eerily still lake with the villain. But Laila and I had no choice. We had to figure out who tried to murder Chef Remi by the time we left Sunderland tomorrow night. After that, we'd have no access to the scene of the crime or to the other competitors. My shot at writing an investigative piece that would prove to myself and the scholarship committee that I had potential would have slipped through my fingers and, worse, we wouldn't be able to clear Laila's name.

I shoved my notebook into my backpack. Next to me, Laila grabbed a rolling pin, and the air actually whistled when she took a powerful test swing.

At least I knew she could take care of herself. I, on the other hand, wished I at least knew the best way to menacingly wield a wooden spoon.

As Laila joined the rest of the competitors for lunch—turkey sandwiches, from the smell of it—I tightened the backpack straps around my shoulders and headed back into the kitchen arena. It was creepy being in here alone. Laila was keeping an eye on everyone else while I tried to figure out what was going on with these cameras. The plan was to compare notes at dinner, after she won round four.

I left the kitchen lights off and switched on my cell phone flashlight instead. Between that and the flashes of lightning, I easily tiptoed around the workstations to reach the camera behind the judges' table.

First thing to check: that these devices actually worked. I would've felt awfully silly pointing fingers if it turned out the Golden Cookie people actually just bought a bunch of buggy cameras in bulk. I picked up the camera and traced its power cord back.

The "You've got to be kidding me" escaped me before I knew it. The camera wasn't plugged into a power source. No connection to the wall or to a USB port of a computer. And because this webcam was the exact model as Dad's, I knew these weren't the fancy ones that are battery operated. No plug-in meant no power, but for how long? What this meant, though, was that it was possible that no one outside this building had any idea what was happening during key parts of day one, despite the school administrators promising everyone's parents that their kids were only a click away.

But the storm and the fact that the connections even froze and dropped throughout our Zoom call with the parents probably had everyone convinced that this was a simple technological glitch, not an intentional act. They were all more focused on the fact that their kids witnessed a crime than the state of the school's internet connection anyway.

I lowered the camera back in its spot and pieced together what I knew. Someone placed this camera here before the competition started and pointed it at the workstations so it'd have a perfect view of everyone. Then they didn't bother to finish the simple setup, or they secretly unplugged the camera at some point and tucked the power cord behind it to make it look like it was set up properly. That evil someone might have figured, as Laila pointed out, that we'd all be way too busy to double-check this detail. It had to be someone here for the competition: there hadn't been anyone else at the school other than the competitors, the judges, the competition coordinator, and the investigators.

The thought—and the crack of thunder outside—sent a chill down my spine.

It took only a few minutes to check the other two cameras. Sure enough, they were positioned in plain view but with their power cords leading to nowhere. Someone put a lot of work into fooling all of us.

Suddenly, I was all too aware I was alone in this room: a room where someone was almost killed less than twenty-four hours ago. Lightning flashed again before the room settled into sinister shadows. I glanced at the clock on my cell phone. The competitors would be finishing up their lunches and returning to the kitchen arena soon. I had to leave before anyone got back. As much as I loved watching Laila bake—and enjoying the delicious results—I couldn't afford to be trapped in here for another two hours.

I had more work to do. I pulled out my notebook and jotted down a list. First, I needed to figure out where the school's security room was. I was willing to bet that the school had some security cameras installed too, at least at the main entrances. These cameras wouldn't have all the in-kitchen angles we needed, but it might help us figure out what Chef Remi was doing all day and if anyone was slinking around him or anywhere else when they weren't supposed to.

Then if I could somehow get a reliable cell phone signal, I might be able to load the Golden Cookie website and social media pages to see if anyone had posted any comments about the camera feed.

I also needed to check in with my parents and maybe even Laila's mom. I needed to calm them down after that disaster of a video call. I didn't want them to worry about us too much, because if anyone called for the cancellation of the competition, it'd tank my and Laila's chances of coming to Sunderland together. Plus, knowing I had a connection to the outside world would make me feel a whole lot better about being stuck here.

Because there was a would-be murderer here at Sunderland.

Until we figured out who it was, we were all in danger.

And we were all suspects.

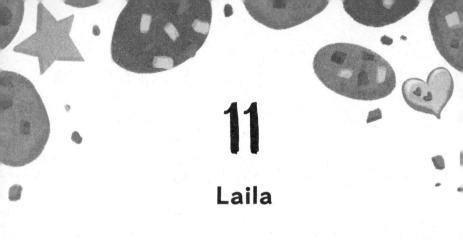

11

Laila

MY STOMACH WAS in knots as they served turkey and veggie sandwiches.

After a quick trip to the bathroom to investigate Jaden's bottle—it held no clues as to what medicine it held or what it was meant to help with, especially with the torn label—all I could think about was Lucy. I hoped she was okay. But worrying about it made the knots knottier, so I shoved a sandwich in my mouth to distract myself.

Flavors burst on my tongue, none of them good. First, I could taste stale bread that absorbed the moisture of the turkey. Second, the lettuce was limp, like eating paper. My superpower kicked into gear. These sandwiches were made almost two days ago. The only reason they were edible was that someone lightly slathered one piece of bread with a sharp, acidic pesto to keep the flavor fresh.

As if that someone knew we'd be stuck inside, unable to get food during this weekend.

I stared off out the windows as the storm raged outside. The trees bent in the wind, rain pelted the glass, thunder rumbled through the sky and floor, and every few seconds lightning flashed. It was normal to get storms like this along the coast of North Carolina. Maybe Chef Noah or Polly expected as much and made these sandwiches in case. Maybe I shouldn't spend too much time thinking about it or anything else beyond the competition . . . which I was losing.

There was a chance I could pull out of my downward spiral. I *could* still win. *There's nowhere you can't go. Nothing you can't do,* I heard my dad tell me. But to win, everything I did from here on out had to be perfect.

Just then, Micah plopped down at my table, and I let out a startled yelp, followed by a "Huh?"

"I never thought you tried to kill Chef Remi," he said before taking a bite of his sandwich. "Of all the people here . . . you'd be my last suspect."

"Your father definitely seemed to think I was the only suspect." I leaned forward, my voice falling to a whisper. "But what do you mean?"

Micah leaned forward too. He smelled like the spices he used in his cookies. I wished suddenly that I had tried them, because unlike mine, they were winners and everyone raved about them. I couldn't lose focus, even though his mighty arms were very distracting and very close.

"Ask them. Philippa's family worked with Chef Remi and Jaden's dads were on that show about Chef Remi traveling the world and eating foods from different cultures." Micah sipped his soda.

"Wait, I saw an episode of that show! He went to Charleston to understand Gullah Geechee food and ended up fighting with everyone about how French food was better. I watched it with . . ." I trailed off. I watched it with Dad. It was so long ago, but I remembered the way he yelled at the TV. My dad said it was like watching someone disrespect his own mother, who was from the same area, who made the same food from the same culture. She had passed away before I ever got to learn it.

I set that memory aside and considered Jaden and Philippa. Jaden could be behind the cameras being off: with professional cameramen for parents, he had to be an expert with that kind of equipment. I bet he helped on his dads' documentaries. And Philippa . . . Besides the knife and possible family connection, there was the way she and Maeve had been sneaking around together. Those two had been keeping secrets. Something was up there. Not to mention they were in the walk-in fighting that first day. Hmm. . . .

"What about Maeve?" I wondered, my lips pinched.

"I only know that their empire was tangled up with Chef Remi once." Micah put his can down on the table, and he leaned in, his voice softer. "They are *all* tangled up with Chef Remi. Especially Noah."

"Well, yeah, he's Remi's assistant," I muttered. I mean, he *was* walking around and helping out and now he was a judge, but it seemed weird I didn't know much about him. Really weird. Though I guess he never did get his chance at foodie fame and fortune the way Remi and Polly had. My lips pursed while my head tilted to the side. "How do you know all of this?"

Micah shrugged again. "A few weeks ago, there was a big banquet celebrating restaurant owners in our district. Everyone was there, even Jaden's dads, who were shooting promo material for the restaurant association. . . . Anyway, I'm not really good at socializing, so I walked around listening. Adults are always so into themselves that they don't usually notice me, so they said whatever they wanted to. It was kinda cool."

I couldn't ask what else he learned because now I knew the truth—everyone but me could have had a reason to want Remi dead. This might not have been about disliking him, it might've been about revenge. But how could Lucy and I find out about how the others were connected when we barely had time between matches as it was?

Wait. Why was Micah telling me all this? He wouldn't spill everything if he had tried to kill Chef Remi himself, would he? Was he trying to distract me? I had no idea how to politely ask, "Hey, did *you* do it?" Lucy would press me to ask if she were here sitting with us.

Our suspect pool had grown. Actually, if what Micah said was all true . . .

One of the could-be murderers was here, in this cafeteria, and he was looking right at me.

Well, not looking so much as scowling.

Jaden. That could be the only explanation. Tech-whiz, camera-tampering Jaden pointed his finger at me right away to avoid anyone looking in his direction. Everyone heard he had issues with his parents too, so maybe he or they were doing something they weren't supposed to. Worse, Chef Remi ate his cookies right before he had mine. He had that baggie in the walk-in and I found his empty medicine bottle too. It could have been poisonous to Chef Remi, could've messed with his heart medicine. None of this could be a coincidence.

I just . . . I was going to have to prove it was him . . . somehow.

"Hey." I tapped Micah's hand. "Thanks for telling me. It's nice to know you didn't believe the worst," I said genuinely. It *was* nice. Micah didn't have to say anything, he could've left me spiraling. And maybe he was telling me this to distract me from thinking he was a suspect too. I didn't know, yet I still appreciated it. "I think you're talented. And I don't know . . . I kinda wish we could've met before the competition."

He smiled and his cheeks turned a bit rosy. "Yeah, me too. You're really cool."

"Thanks," I said, my own cheeks heating a little bit. I was thinking about what I would say next when Chef Polly's voice cut through the room.

"So that was a whopper of a first round for the day, huh? We had some real winners . . ." She beamed at Micah. "And some not-so-great entries." Her gaze flitted to mine, and Jaden laughed obnoxiously. At least Philippa, Maeve, and Micah didn't join in. "While Chef Noah"—and that's when I noticed she'd started calling him Chef—"is busy preparing the room for the next challenge, I get to announce what you're going to be doing."

She smiled and everyone perked up, waiting and thrumming their fingers against the table. When she saw the anticipation wash through us, she continued like a true television host.

"Since Micah was the winner and has the coveted advantage, you're all at his mercy!" Chef Polly giggled. "He can choose to make you work in teams . . ." She waggled her eyebrows. "Or pick an ingredient that only he's proficient in using to throw you all off. So, Micah, what do you say?"

A light bulb flickered in my mind. This was my opening; it would be my chance to investigate Jaden. He couldn't brush me off, not if he was stuck working beside me.

"Teams," I whispered. Micah gave me an odd face, and I nodded once to tell him I was serious. Yes, we just established our friendship, and yes, I was asking a lot, but it was super important.

He sat up and fiddled his fingers, which must have been a nervous habit. "I choose teams. Um . . ."

"Together," I whispered again, drawing a curious glance from Maeve.

"Ms. Laila, you aren't telling Micah what to do, are you?" Chef Polly narrowed her gaze on me.

"No, ma'am," I said sweetly before turning back to Micah.

I tilted my head in the direction of Jaden, and lacing my fingers together, I mimicked the concept of together. Micah stared at me, puzzled, before mouthing, "Really?"

I nodded once again and turned back to Polly as if I were being totally normal and not telling him what to do at all. Chef Polly didn't look convinced.

"Maeve and Philippa on one team, Jaden and Laila on

another. And they have to be bound together." Micah said it with a smile, like that was what I meant. Yes, I wanted to work with Jaden to find out how he could've hurt Chef Remi . . . but being physically tied to him?

Jaden pinned me with a glare. "I don't want to work with a criminal."

"Neither do I," I said with my head held high. Jaden's scowl disappeared and his brows raised. Philippa and Maeve chittered.

"There are no criminals here," Polly said firmly. Then she continued as if we hadn't spoken. "Sounds like fun! Like a three-legged race at the county fair. Are you all ready to get in that kitchen and bake?"

Philippa and Maeve shared a smile, one that reached their eyes and loosened their shoulders. They were clearly closer than they let on, more than two people who were in after-school clubs together or whatever. Seeing them made me wish that Lucy were here, that I could share everything I'd learned with her. That I could have her support and her wisdom. And a hug. I think I needed a hug.

Once we were in the kitchen, though, a hug was the last thing on my mind. Instead, it was regret. I never should have pushed Micah to do this. While he excitedly leaned against his own bench, I was stuck at Jaden's. There was a long, thick strand of kitchen twine in front of us. This was going to be epically bad.

"Now, contestants, you've got to be tied around the arms," Polly said with a little laugh. "No one break your twine, okay? If you do, you'll have to be disqualified for the round."

"Remember, this is still a cookie competition," Noah added. "Bound or not, you have to make us something truly delectable. Something from your past, that tastes like home, or that honors someone who inspires you in the kitchen. Got it?"

"Yes, Chef!" we all said.

"Oh, this is going to be a hoot!" Polly clapped. "Ready, set, bake!"

Jaden turned to stare at me, his lips curled. "We should tie it around your right arm and my left."

"No way, I'm right-handed." I put a hand on my hip. Being bound to would-be murderer Jaden wasn't going to be "a hoot" and I didn't want to rely completely on him to succeed. I watched Maeve and Philippa get bound together at the other station and they seemed rather happy with the idea.

"So what? I'm stronger than you." Jaden rolled his eyes.

I scoffed. "You wish."

"We're wasting time." Jaden sighed, drumming his fingers on the table. "The millionaire's shortbread I want to make takes a half hour to set. I want to win, don't you? So let's get this over with."

Drat! That was actually reasonable coming from Jaden. I *did* want to win, and wasting time would definitely ruin the chances of that. But I also wanted to investigate. I'd have to somehow do both, which meant focusing and using my time wisely.

Chef Noah stepped up to our bench expectantly. "This is a tough pairing and I hope you'll move past your differences and work together. Are you ready?"

"Fine," I muttered as he tied up my left arm and Jaden's right. And then, for extra humiliation, he bound our feet together too, adding that if any two contestants could break the rope out of sheer frustration, it was us.

As soon as he left, Jaden yanked me toward the walk-in. He grabbed things and shoved them into my chest and I struggled to hold it all. I barely had time to catch my breath, set everything down, and figure out my own cookies when he tugged me downward near the flour bins back at our table. When I bent over like him, I noticed his head down, eyes closed. "What are you doing?"

"Nothing," he muttered angrily. Still, he didn't stop bending over. Sweat beaded along his scalp. He was either in pain or nervous. No, not nervous, guilty—I was sure of it. "I need a moment."

I may not have had Lucy's observational skills, but I still knew this was *the* moment to inquire about his motive. There was the right way to approach this or the wrong way. I went with the quickest. "I heard your dads worked with Chef Remi . . . and it didn't end well?"

Jaden's eyes tore open and his gaze landed on mine. He didn't say anything as he stood, jerking me upward too. He plucked the handheld grater from the bench and began zesting an orange. His actions were frantic. The zest flopped out of the bowl and scattered all over the other ingredients. It set me a little on edge, and I almost wished I hadn't brought the entire thing up. I wasn't Lucy. I could figure out all the flavor components in a fancy dessert, but I couldn't figure out people. Not like her.

I tried to backtrack. "Jaden, I'm—"

"You're the last person I want to work with." His shoulders were tensed high and he placed an orange down so hard, juice trickled onto the bench. "You might try to kill me if I get in your way like you did with Chef Remi—"

"Hey!" I whispered harshly, reaching for my bag of hazelnuts. "From what I heard, it could have been you. Chef Remi worked with your dads, right? Maybe *you* wanted him dead."

"Oh yeah, who told you that? Micah? I bet he didn't say what Chef Remi did to his parents, did he?" Jaden sneered, but there was some conflicting emotion swimming in his eyes too. I had a feeling I upset him. . . . "He's a jerk, and so are you."

Anger surged through me and I ripped the bag of hazelnuts, sending them cascading along the bench and onto the floor. "All you do is whine and accuse me of cheating because you know I'm as good as you or better. You're the jerk."

Jaden shook his head, stepping closer to me. I refused to shrink. Besides, we were bound together; I couldn't cower even if I wanted to. "I'm not a jerk, and I didn't try to kill Chef Remi. Why don't we taste my cookies and you'll see. Chef Polly locked them in the cafeteria kitchen to hand over to the police once the roads clear."

I jutted my chin out, splaying my hand down firmly on the wooden bench. "No way. The almond flour was bad. Your macarons were disgusting—"

"You think I would bake with rancid almond flour? Nice try." Jaden laughed and it sent tingles up my spine. "I took the package you handed me back to my bench and tossed it. I also noticed you switch out the sabotaged egg whites. That's why you're a jerk."

I cringed, and the attitude in my voice slipped a bit. "Why didn't you tell someone?"

"Because I was being a jerk too," he admitted. The fluorescent lights overhead flickered brighter, and Jaden flinched as if it caused him pain. "My macarons were perfect. Try them. I dare you."

"Fine. But we should try mine too." I took a half step forward, daring him to back down. "It's the least you could do since you've been mean to me the entire time I've been here, shoved me, called me names, and kept accusing me of everything from cheating to murder."

Jaden was so close, his nose almost touched mine. "Maybe it's because that judge knew you at the competition and handed you the win."

"I—"

He shook his head as I attempted to lie. He was right. I didn't deserve to win only because the judge knew me. But there was nothing I could do about that, and I had to believe my baking was still good enough for that win—Lucy thought so.

"Some of us only have baking. We don't have judges in our corner or friends tagging along for support." His shoulders sagged. When he spoke again, his words were soft, almost pleading. "Try the macaron, you'll see I'm innocent."

"And you'll try mine?"

He nodded, his lips pressed into a grim line. "Yeah."

"Fine."

"Fine." He stepped back finally, his movements oddly slow. "Now can we bake? If we want to win, we need to make at least three cookies to beat them, though they hardly look like they can concentrate long enough to bake."

I followed his line of sight to Philippa and Maeve, who were smiling adoringly at each other. Maeve scribbled something down on a recipe card in front of her, and Philippa giggled. Philippa. I couldn't put my finger on it, but they had a deep bond. Maybe a bond strong enough to commit murder together? I wasn't sure, yet I did know they were hiding something.

Hm. Then again, it seemed *everyone* here was hiding, something except me and Lucy. Any one of the other contestants could be the potential murderer. . . . Though I was beginning to worry it might not be Jaden.

12

Lucy

THE BASEMENT AIR was disgustingly warm and musty, like the locker room after PE. The last place I wanted to be was alone in an isolated corner of an empty building, in the middle of a storm. And with a potential killer loose?

Nope.

My speed walk turned into a jog.

I clutched the wooden spoon I'd taken from the kitchen. If anyone jumped out at me, I was ready to . . . well, whatever someone did with a wooden spoon. I would probably brandish this thing and make big, threatening noises to scare off my attacker. Everyone else was locked up in the kitchen arena, suffering from whatever round four had in store for them. So if I met anyone down in this basement, they'd no doubt be up to no good.

I scanned the nameplates on each of the doors as I ran by.

There were a few offices down here, but it was mostly storage. Then I saw it: security. This must have been where the monitors for all the security cameras were. I'd swept every other floor in this building (my PE-hating legs were killing me, by the way) and hadn't found anything. If this room wasn't the hub of all the security cameras here, then I didn't know where that hub was. There was a chance that the security footage fed to somewhere off campus, but with the electricity and the wireless signal so spotty, I really hoped that wasn't the case.

Because that would've meant there was a chance that no one, anywhere, saw what happened to Chef Remi.

I tried the door and groaned aloud: it was locked.

I angled and bumped my shoulder against the door. Then I bumped again, harder. Nothing. It didn't budge.

I blew out a breath into the already icky air. I didn't love the idea of breaking into the room, but I told myself it was for worthy causes: Laila's innocence and my journalism career. Watching that security footage was a matter of the greater good.

The timer on my phone buzzed, and I frowned. I told Laila I'd make it back to the kitchen arena in time to see her win round four. I didn't have time to pick the door's lock—which I didn't even know how to do anyway. But maybe there was a tool up in the kitchen that could help Laila and me jimmy this thing open tonight. Or maybe someone upstairs knew where the key to the security room was. I could ask around. Noah was in contact with the school administrators. He might be able to help us contact someone who could get us access to the security footage from yesterday.

Heading back empty-handed was partially a win: I did find the security room, after two hours of running through every single hallway here. It was like when Ariella Wilborn tracked down a fugitive drug kingpin at a resort in Mazatlán but couldn't get past the guards. What did she do? That night, she booked the most expensive suite in the resort— conveniently in the same wing as the kingpin's—for her and her camera crew. Her story led to the kingpin's arrest and a dozen awards for Ariella.

I could see my future now: *Junior high journalist and baker-extraordinaire bestie expose would-be killer at cookie competition. School thanks them with guaranteed admission, free tuition, and the biggest, best dorm on campus. Ariella Wilborn brings journalist on as the youngest-ever coanchor on a prime-time cable news show, and they go on to win every investigative journalism award in the world. Twice.*

Okay, some of that was a stretch. But it kept my mind on the prize as I dashed back to the kitchen arena. I paused to catch my breath before entering. Peering through the high windows in the door, I saw Micah at his workstation alone but then all the other competitors paired up with ropes tying them together. I smoothed down my hair and pushed the double doors open with my fingertips just slightly enough for me to slip in. Noah spotted me, pursed his lips, then motioned for me to take my seat. Whatever story Laila spun for him, it must've been convincing.

I quietly slid my heavy backpack off my shoulder and tried to catch Laila's eye to cheer her on. It was then that I noticed she was paired up with Jaden, and they both seemed to be moving around jerkily and off-center. It was worse than I thought: they were literally tied to each other with kitchen twine.

After pulling out my DSLR camera, I snapped a few more pictures of the competitors. I paid special attention to the corners of the room so Laila and I could go over every tiny detail later. There might have been some clues that we overlooked: something in the kitchen that wasn't supposed to be here or something missing entirely.

"Do you want to announce the time, Noah?" Chef Polly asked Noah. They were posted up in front of my workstation, and they seemed to have forgotten that I was there: neither had spoken to me after I'd entered late. Without making a sound, I lowered my camera and leaned in to listen.

"*Chef* Noah," he corrected.

She gave the slightest indignant *humph*, the same sound I would've made if I weren't so worried about them noticing I was behind them, eavesdropping. "Doing all the paperwork to open a restaurant doesn't quite make you a chef."

Noah glowered. "I'll have you know I trained in Japan. My ramen restaurant would've blown everyone else out of the water here."

That surprised me: Noah, an actual chef? And Chef Remi had been treating him like his own personal butler, chauffeur, scheduler—anything but an actual kitchen colleague.

"I'll believe it when you invite me to the ribbon cutting," Chef Polly said. She had a way of saying mean things in a sweet voice so you weren't ever sure if she was being purposefully cruel. But I heard the steel in her voice: she meant it. She didn't seem to respect Noah one bit. "You are expecting to open sometime soon, right?"

The squeaky way Noah said "yes" totally meant "no."

"All I need is to get some last funding lined up. Some issues with an investor, you know how that is. . . ." He trailed off, glancing down at his watch before bellowing, "One more minute, competitors! Put those finishing touches on your pieces."

While the competitors whirled around, I quietly picked up my pen and jotted down some notes about Noah's restaurant dreams and how Polly seemed to think herself above him. Finally, Noah called an end to the round. Jaden was a blur of movement as he ripped off the kitchen twine, like he couldn't get away from Laila fast enough. By the curl of Laila's snarl, she felt the same way. I was sure I'd hear all about this forced partnership tonight over dinner. But for now, I shoved every other thought in my mind aside and focused on our possible suspects. Jaden was at the opposite side of the workstation from Laila, as if he'd chosen to ignore her existence. He was trying a little too hard to distance himself from her, and he was the first one to point a finger at her as a possible suspect in what happened to Chef Remi. What's that saying? He who smelt it, dealt it?

Over at the other workstation, Philippa was back to her whispering ways. She stood close to Maeve, muttering something that I probably wouldn't be able to hear even if I were standing next to them. She seemed too good at this. Too good at keeping secrets. And the way she was glaring at Laila and Jaden's workstation? Was this just an overcompetitive spirit, or was it something more?

Chef Polly and Noah made their way through the workstations.

First up was Micah. "Oatmeal cookie sandwiches?" Noah asked with an eyebrow raised. "Playing it safe again, eh?"

Now it was my turn to raise an eyebrow. I caught a hint of something snarky in Noah's tone. It actually made me think of Chef Remi. Noah had been nothing but nice to me since we arrived. But maybe his interaction with Chef Polly earlier had put him in a bad mood.

Chef Polly finished her bite of Micah's cookie. "My word, these do seem rather safe, but that filling! And brown butter! Marvelous."

Micah beamed, Laila bit her lip, and my heart dropped. I so wanted her to win. She needed this to stay competitive for the Golden Cookie.

Next, the chefs moved on to Laila and Jaden. True to the overachievers that both of them were, they had baked three cookies.

Laila smiled before waving at the plate of her powdered-sugar-covered cookies like she was a game show host. "We've made our favorites and worked together to create a cookie that blends our flavors. So we've got my Italian hazelnut–orange cookies, Jaden's millionaire's shortbread, and finally, these chocolate-dipped Florentines."

"Three? So ambitious," Chef Polly said. She complimented Laila's and Jaden's individual cookies, then her eyes widened when she took a bite of a Florentine. "Oh my."

Noah nibbled at a Florentine and smiled. "I'm catching

some notes of ginger and orange in there. This is quite a sophisticated flavor for you two."

Huh. Another weird-sounding comment. *For you two.* Maybe I was reading too much into it, but Noah seemed to have stepped into this chef judge role too seriously. Maybe he wouldn't be up for helping us bend the rules to get into the security room after all.

"What inspired these?" Chef Polly asked. I suspected she was asking to stall while she ate another cookie from each plate, for fun.

Laila opened her mouth to answer, but Jaden beat her to it.

"The millionaire's shortbread is my g-ma's recipe," he said. "Her new husband doesn't like that my dads are married, so he's found reasons to keep G-ma from visiting us every Christmas like she used to. The flu, some appointment he can't miss, the flu again, whatever. But that hasn't kept her from sending our family a whole box of Christmas cookies. These are for her."

I blinked. So Jaden did have a heart. Or, before I sympathized with the enemy too much, his g-ma had a heart. He just got to reap the benefits every Christmas.

Chef Polly fanned a tear away. "That's lovely, Jaden. And you, Laila?"

I knew the answer to this one, and it made me smile as she answered.

"My mom doesn't do peanut butter anymore. She's not allergic or anything, but for a few months after Dad died, all we ate was PB and Js, so now she can't stand the taste. She was craving something nutty one day, so I dug up this Italian hazelnut–orange cookie recipe, tweaked it a little, and now she asks for it all the time."

Noah patted her on the shoulder. "So the orange from your cookie and the milk chocolate from Jaden's made it into this Florentine."

If I expected Laila and Jaden to be proud of how they set aside their differences to work together, I was wrong.

Jaden snorted. "Well, I wanted pistachios in the Florentines."

Laila rolled her eyes. "And I'm telling you, again, it would've been over-the-top."

"Over-the-top? Have you seen what you're wearing? They could spot your shirt from space."

Noah chose that moment to usher Chef Polly over to Philippa and Maeve, which was for the best. The longer Jaden and Laila fought with each other, the more likely it was that she'd bop him over the head with her rolling pin and get disqualified.

Their bickering masked the judges' assessments of Philippa and Maeve's work. They had made only one type of cookie: bright purple ube crinkles.

Noah scrunched his nose. "You had plenty of time to do more than one cookie, girls."

Maeve's lip trembled.

Chef Polly shook her head. "It's a shame, because these crinkles are splendid. That ube flavor, that vivid color. But it does make me wonder what you two were doing all this time if you weren't baking. You must remember you're here to compete. And if the other competitor pair made three cookies . . ." She ended with a shrug.

Chef Polly made a good point. I committed that to memory so I could jot it down in my notebook later: Philippa and Maeve might've been up to something earlier in round four, when I was downstairs. Hiding evidence, maybe? Everyone was still a suspect—though Philippa was a lot higher up on that list—and Laila might have some info to fill in those gaps in Philippa and Maeve's time later.

For now, I sent all my positive energy Laila's way as Chef Polly and Noah chatted off to the side. After this morning's disaster, she needed this win.

Chef Polly turned to the competitors. "We've made a decision. The winners of this round are—"

"Jaden and Laila!" Noah cut in.

I must've let out a hoot because everyone turned to me. I shrank down in my seat as the competitors began to clean up.

"You have an hour break before dinner," Chef Polly said. "But we've spoken to the Sunderland administrators, and they've ordered that you not leave your rooms after seven tonight."

"What? Another curfew?" Philippa practically shrieked.

Not that I wanted to get stuck in our room either, but Philippa was awfully angry for someone who shouldn't have anywhere to go after seven anyway.

Noah nodded. "It's for your safety. I'm sure you all understand."

"But my workout!" Micah groaned.

Laila smoothed down her apron. "Safety? Does . . . do people think I'm a criminal again? I can lock myself in—"

Chef Polly shook her head. "No, no, honey. We've heard nothing further from the doctors or law enforcement, but this is Sunderland's competition and their administrators make the rules. And since that nice Detective Valdez can't get on campus because of the roads, it's best to follow those rules, okay?"

My jaw tightened. I couldn't believe the adults were

continuing to hide the truth about the foul play from us. I got that they didn't want us to panic, but did they really think we wouldn't wonder why they were locking us in our rooms tonight?

A few more grumbles floated through the room, and I headed over to Laila once Jaden slung his apron over his shoulder and left.

I pulled her into a quick, almond-extract-scented hug. "Congratulations! I knew you'd bounce back."

"Thanks. That means I've won two rounds, but Jaden and Micah are close behind." She sighed. "If I don't win the Golden Cookie . . ."

"Hey, you will. You're in the lead, and you'll do great tomorrow, I know it."

She smiled before leaning in and lowering her voice. "So, what'd you find?"

I told her about the security room, sliding the wooden spoon back into the workstation drawer when no one was looking. "But this whole curfew business throws a wrench into the plan for both of us to find a way in there tonight. I'm going to have to open the door tomorrow while you're all competing. I have no clue how I'm going to do this by myself."

I sighed, the last bits of my confidence going with it. My

partial win seemed to have turned into a defeat after all.

Laila peered around her workstation, then started fishing for something in a canister of kitchen tools. "Well then, it's a good thing we're stuck inside together all night, with no distractions. Because you, my friend, are going to learn how to pick a lock and I have *lots* to tell you. Including my plan."

LAILA'S JOURNAL ENTRY

List of suspects:

Jaden: his dads worked with Chef Remi. He could've been the one to stop the live streaming cameras. Also, he's evil. Definitely a villain. Obnoxiously talented too. Okay, maybe not a full-blown villain. I think he's lonely. Plus, he knows I tried to sabotage him but didn't tell anyone. So he can't be completely evil. Still, we have to watch him.

Philippa: her parents worked with Chef Remi. Also, she brought in an illegal knife, which Lucy thinks suggests she's a rule breaker. Also, what is up with her and Maeve?

Maeve: her parents know Chef Remi . . . no idea how. She's a science whiz who could've concocted a poison that nearly killed Chef Remi. Also, what is up with her and Philippa?

Chef Polly: really hates Chef Remi. She acts suspicious, but she's not tech savvy and she's very frail.

Chef Noah: ??? None of us know much about him other than he worked with Chef Remi for a long time and never got promoted. He seems nice actually, though he has been weirdly distracted the entire time.

micah the mighty: extremely cute. Loves to exercise and has such a kind heart. According to Jaden, Chef Remi did something to his parents, but Jaden would say anything to blame someone else. Loves plants—could he have brought a poisonous plant to school and slipped a leaf into one of his cookies? Unlikely. I mean, he is SO CUTE. . . . But then even the prettiest of roses have thorns.

Me: very ambitious but wasn't supposed to be a competitor this weekend. Has absolutely no motive since I was winning day one anyway. However, all the parents believe I did it and the police might too. . . . Not good.

Lucy: no motive. No means. Didn't make a cookie that Chef Remi nearly choked on. Also, very ambitious but not in a murdery type of way.

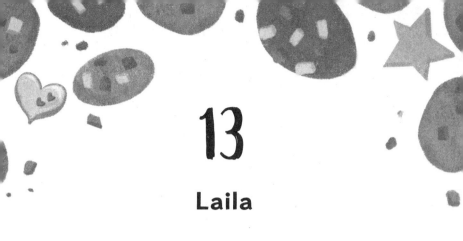

13

Laila

IT WAS ALMOST ten p.m., and I'd spent a few hours teaching Lucy to pick a lock. It was just the thing I needed to improve my mood, especially after being tied up to Jaden. And also because it reminded me of Dad.

I learned lockpicking when he died. He had a file cabinet full of important documents, and Mom couldn't find the key. So I watched some videos and got good at it. When I finally opened the cabinet, I found clippings of recipes he had saved for me and a gigantic folder full of all the pictures I drew as a kid. All sorts of portraits of our family, our house, and us cooking together.

Thinking about it, I had to twist my lips not to cry a little. To snap out of it, I shared every hint Micah told me about the other competitors.

"That's very suspicious," Lucy admitted as she fluffed her pillow. "And why would he tell you all of that?"

"Because he wants to be friends and he trusts me . . . ," I said, trailing off. It sounded flimsy to my own ears.

"You're letting your emotions cloud your judgment. He might have told you what you wanted to hear so you wouldn't think he's a suspect." Lucy looked over at me from her twin bed. "We should question him tomorrow. And Jaden . . . nice job finding a way to investigate him. Creative. What did you learn? What was it like working with him?" Her voice traveled across the small dorm room. She may have been all pajamaed and tucked in for the night, but she was still bending bobby pins like I showed her.

I stared at the wall clock. Tomorrow was the final day. Winning the last challenge (with Jaden) meant I was at the top of the competition, yet it didn't mean I'd win the whole thing. I had an edge, but I also knew the competition better too.

"If you don't listen to all the mean things he says and you forget about everything bad he's done, you'll be amazed by how talented he is. Like . . ." I shook my head, remembering how he tasted the cookie dough and added another dash of extract that really made the whole thing pop. "If I didn't loathe him, I'd want to be his friend. I think he needs friends, I think he doesn't know how to talk to people. He could be a cool person if he had a better attitude."

"Hmmm . . . ," Lucy said, burrowing farther under her Sunderland blanket.

"Anyway, I thought working with him would make it easier for me to figure out if he tried to kill Chef Remi or not. But—" I yawned and my eyes blinked slowly. "But . . ." Another yawn claimed me. "It didn't. If he did it, he'd have to be a genius with great time-management skills, and he might be." I was talking nonsense then. I had no idea if Jaden did it. I'd try his cookie tomorrow. Polly ate them and she was fine—the same could be said for my cookies too, a fact everyone seemingly overlooked—so we already knew that whatever almost killed Chef Remi wasn't poison. Much as I loathed him, something in my gut told me it wasn't him. "And I have a feeling that the secret bag he had . . . isn't what caused Chef Remi to choke. I think it was chamomile tea. It's weird, I know. . . ."

Lucy didn't respond, and I was sure she was already fast asleep. I joined her soon after, having a vivid nightmare about Chef Remi coughing up cookie bits in the kitchen arena. He twisted around to look at me and choked out, "You!"

I shook my head and waved my hands. My mouth tried to say, "No, I didn't do it," yet no words came out. Tears streamed down my face. Behind him, Chef Polly clutched her pearls and Noah laughed. The rest of the contestants pointed at me. "Murderer," they said. But I wasn't.

One of *them* was. Micah the Mighty could be one. And being too trusting during a baking competition was a sure-fire way to get burned.

LUCY'S JOURNAL ENTRY

Checklist of things to pack for Sunday investigation:

  Phone

  Pen

  Notebook

  Bobby pins (as many as Laila can spare—will need extra, just in case)

  Wooden spoon or some other kind of protection

  Hoodie (this building gets so cold!)

DAY THREE

EAT SWEET OR DIE BITTER

14

Laila

LUCY SHOOK MY shoulder till I woke up. The rain was still pelting the windows hard, but there was light in the room. The sun found a way to shine through all those dark clouds, which was what I needed to do too.

"Time to get up. Today's the day," she said somberly.

It was going to be a long day: first, I'd have to sample the cookies that might nearly have killed Chef Remi, then we'd have to solve a possible murder, and in the meantime, I would have to bake something that would decide if we went to Sunderland together.

I knew that was a lot to juggle, but I was mainly thinking about me and Lucy. If we separated now, I wondered if there would be common activities between our passions for cooking and journalism that'd keep us together across the distance. Or if we'd slowly drift apart. Who would I be without my best friend? What would I do on my own?

I groaned into my pillow. "I don't want to get up."

"Hey." Lucy took a seat on the mattress beside me. "You're going to win. I'm going to get a scholarship for Sunderland. We'll share a room like this one. It'll be awesome."

I rolled over and looked at her. Her pajamas had notebooks and pen illustrations all over them. There was hope swimming in my best friend's wide-eyed gaze. I wanted to believe her. We went together like pizza and cheese, peanut butter and jelly, chocolate chip cookies and a sprinkle of sea salt.

When my dad died, Lucy sat on one side and Mom on the other in the church at the funeral. She held my hand as my head fell on her shoulder. When I was waiting for the results of my first cooking competition in second grade, Lucy was cheering the loudest in the audience. And when I had a hard time getting out of bed the summer Dad and I had planned to go on a road trip to see the Culinary Institute of America in New York, Lucy cut out tons of pictures of the place and taped them to my walls.

Here she was now, believing in me and telling me I could do this. I couldn't let her down. I slowly sat up and wrapped my arms around her in a big, necessary hug.

She laughed. "What's that for?"

"Thanks for being my best friend," I said softly. "Thanks for being here with me."

She sighed. "I wouldn't miss this for the world. Although this probably would've been nicer if we hadn't witnessed someone almost die."

I let my arms fall from her as I scooted to the edge of the bed beside her. "Right. But we're here together, and we're going to solve who tried to kill Chef Remi. And if I lose and we don't go to Sunderland together"—I swallowed hard because it was painful uttering those words—"at least we did the right thing. Assuming the police don't arrest me too, but it's best not to think about that."

"Yeah," Lucy agreed. "We're going to try our hardest, that's all we can do."

I stood up and held a hand out to her. "Let's go be brave and talented."

"Everything feels so much more serious." She took my hand and I pulled her up. "Is it just me, or has Noah—"

"Chef Noah," I interrupted.

"Right, Chef Noah. Have you noticed he's different?"

I considered that for a moment as she drifted to her bag to reach for her clothes. "He's different, yeah. He told us to call him Chef Noah, and he's been a little meaner than he used to be. But he's a judge now, so maybe he's being a bit more critical?"

She nodded. "Yeah, that could be one explanation."

"I mean, he was devastated when Chef Remi almost died. I saw him crying yesterday, clutching Chef Remi's heart medicine—I knew it was the medicine because it was the same type of bottle Jaden had." I paused, thinking about that for a moment, until the thought floated away. "He tried so hard to help Chef Remi, but it seems that the chef never listened to anyone. He was probably thinking that if the stubborn chef had taken better care of himself like he was supposed to, he'd be okay today."

Lucy's face pinched. "Chef Remi really was pretty terrible, even to people trying to be nice to him apparently."

We fell into silence as we got dressed, Lucy in her usual hoodie—she wore her neon-pink chocolate-doughnut shirt underneath—and jeans, me in a pair of cookie-and-milk-bottle-printed leggings and a plain tunic that matched the color scheme. My lucky outfit. I dragged my braids back into a bun atop my head with another lucky item: my favorite scrunchie. I was dressed for battle.

Lucy marked off every item in her notebook checklist twice, then we left together, arm in arm. We bumped right into Maeve and Philippa holding hands in the hall. When they saw us, Philippa attempted to pull her hand away but Maeve held tight. Both of them flushed in our presence.

"What . . . what's going on here?" Lucy instantly switched into fact-finding mode. She lifted up her notebook and clicked her pen. I caught the wariness in her words. Maybe she thought something was suspicious about these two competitors being so close, but it didn't *feel* suspicious.

"Nothing," Philippa snapped. "Mind your own business."

Her tone earned her a quiet "Come on, Philippa" from Maeve.

Maeve seemed to squeeze Philippa's hand, and I suddenly pinned what that feeling was. It was like when someone dipped french fries in their milkshake. You wouldn't think it'd work together, but the sweetness and saltiness were delicious. Like how Philippa's boldness and Maeve's timidness paired well too.

There was something they were hiding from us all, but attempted murder?

"You can trust us," I tried.

At that, Maeve's face relaxed. "I . . . I know." She turned to Philippa. "We can be ourselves with Lucy and Laila. They're not going to judge us," Maeve said with a shy smile that she aimed at Lucy and me. She must have seen our confusion, though, because her smile faltered a bit. "We've been dating for the last few months. She's my . . . well, she's my . . ."

Philippa held her head high, her eyes narrowed, her chin jutting out like she dared us to interrupt and say something negative. "I'm her girlfriend."

"Oh," Lucy said. She clicked her pen closed.

"Cool." I shrugged, and then everything came together in that fries-and-milkshake way. The way they were hiding out in the walk-in. The way they'd been inseparable. The way they looked at each other. We knew they were keeping secrets, but this . . . Now that I knew, it made sense. Though I couldn't understand why they didn't tell us.

As if reading my mind, Maeve exhaled slowly. "We were nervous that people wouldn't understand and say we're . . . it's not okay. Philippa's parents are against the whole thing. That's why we both want to go to Sunderland, away from everyone."

"We understand, and we're sorry about jerks who don't get it," Lucy said without missing a beat. "Those people aren't worth your time. I hope your parents will come around."

Maeve sniffled suddenly and Philippa gave something between a scowl and smile.

"Before the next round, we wanted to say, well, we never believed you tried to murder Chef Remi," Maeve said. "I know our parents were terrible on the call, but we don't feel the same. We saw how much it bothered you yesterday and wanted to clear the air so you'd feel better competing. Besides . . . the rest of us . . . well . . . we sorta wanted him dead too. Though we all feel bad about it now."

Another pen click from Lucy. Her notebook was back out too. "Is that why you brought that knife, Philippa?"

Philippa's eyes widened. "Well, yes. I mean, no. I brought my knife with my family name on it to threaten him. But I couldn't go through with it." When I gasped, Philippa rolled her eyes. "Oh, come on. He's the actual worst."

"And you said 'we,' Maeve." Lucy didn't miss a step.

"I didn't bring a knife!"

I raised an eyebrow. Maeve was a science whiz, wasn't she? "We didn't say you brought a knife. Maybe you might've had some other weapons at your disposal."

Lucy held Maeve's gaze. "During the second challenge, you had a bunch of eyedroppers. Those weren't all flavoring extracts, were they?"

Maeve shifted on her feet. "I had planned to spike one of my cookies and give him diarrhea. Something I mixed up in my home lab, no long-term effects or anything. But I couldn't go through with it either. Plus there was no way to do that without hurting Chef Polly too."

Philippa gave a curt wave with her free hand. "None of it matters anyway. Chef Remi had been struggling for years with a heart condition, even back when he was supposed to help with my parents' restaurant. Honestly, if it weren't for Noah, Chef Remi would've kicked the bucket a long time ago. He probably missed his dose of medicine or something. . . . He'll make a full recovery because evil people never die." Maeve must've squeezed her hand again, because Philippa shot her a glance before continuing. "Anyway . . . we should get going. . . ."

"Wait," I blurted out. I couldn't believe I was doing this, but . . . "Earlier, when you said the rest of you 'sorta wanted him dead too' . . . even . . . Micah?"

Maeve and Philippa shared a look but didn't volunteer any more information until Lucy began scrawling furiously in her notebook. They must have worried they were inching back on the suspect list because Maeve answered. "Well, yeah, Chef Remi almost bankrupted his family's restaurant because of an argument, not sure what about—I think it involved a lot of bad reviews. It was a long time ago. . . ."

My heart pounded. Micah didn't mention any of that.

"Can we move this conversation to the cafeteria?" Philippa cut in. "Dinner last night was awful, and I'm starving." Her stomach grumbled, as if to make her point.

"Fine with me," Lucy said, "as long as you're okay with me asking a few follow-up questions."

Right, the cafeteria. I had to find some time to check

out the cafeteria kitchen, where everyone's cookies had been locked in by Chef Polly, as evidence. There could be a clue, I just needed to get in there and figure it out. And it had to be me: Lucy, supersleuth that she was, didn't have the trained palate that I did and wouldn't be able to pick out any suspicious extra ingredients.

We headed to the cafeteria for breakfast together, me and Lucy arm in arm, my mind whirring about how I could get to the cookies, and Maeve and Philippa hand in hand. Thankfully, the spread this morning looked much better than the sad bean-and-cheese burritos from last night. Canned refried beans? How dare.

When Maeve and Philippa went to select a few pastries, Lucy leaned in close to me, her voice low. "Chef Remi didn't miss his medicine like Philippa thinks. Whoever hurt the chef is way too good at covering their tracks and convincing all the adults, and some of the competitors, that everything is fine. But someone turned off the cameras, and I'm going to find out—"

"Hold that thought," I said, wagging my finger while keeping my voice down. "I'm going to investigate the cookies while everyone is busy. This is the best chance I've got."

"Are you sure—" Lucy began, shaking her head.

"We both know there was nothing dangerous in the cookies—only dangerous to Chef Remi. It should be safe.

Besides, Jaden said he would eat them too. He's a jerk—not a jerk with a death wish. I'll be right back." I gestured to the rest of the contestants. "Cover me?"

"I think this is a bad idea," Lucy grumbled, but she stayed right behind Philippa and Maeve to distract them from my hopefully quick absence. "So, I thought of a few follow-up questions," she said to them.

I darted past the empty cereal canisters and the screen used for the Zoom call where everyone hated me and wanted me arrested, past the buffet line, and through the back swinging doors. The clock was ticking, and I needed to find those cookies. My feet squelched on the black-and-white-tiled linoleum in the darkened workspace.

With ginger steps, I tiptoed toward the kitchen refrigerators, listening for someone, anyone, to come in and yell at me.

Yet no one did. I was completely alone, standing in front of the latched refrigerator doors. I used all my might to tug a door open, tamping down a groan when it almost didn't budge. A bright light came on almost immediately and I peeked inside.

On one sheet pan was a smattering of cookies. *Our* cookies. I recognized Maeve's matcha white chocolate sables. Philippa's dark chocolate peanut butter blossoms. Micah's spicy gingersnaps and Jaden's hibiscus-passion-fruit macarons. Beside them were my brown sugar shortbread, triple chocolate filled with white chocolate, and chocolate chip cookies à la Jacques Torres.

My brow furrowed. They looked nearly the same . . . only now they all seemed to be dusted with a powder. Not powdered sugar, something else. Something thinner, not an ingredient I saw in the Sunderland kitchen.

I shook my head. None of us had dusted our cookies with whatever this was. This must've been done after we served them to the judges . . . but why? And who?

This was proof, only I wasn't sure of what yet. I'd have to taste them.

I bent over and gave them a good sniff. The scent lingered in my nose, the smell familiar. I wasn't getting bad vibes from them; if anything, the familiarity gave me confidence that whatever the powder was couldn't be lethal. No, these were safe. Not poisonous. Because logistically, it couldn't be. The detectives said Chef Remi wasn't poisoned, and they would know that by now, right?

Right?

I licked my finger and touched my shortbread. With a quick, sharp inhale, I brought it to my lips.

I couldn't do it.

I had to think. It wasn't poison. It was something that specifically could affect Chef Remi like an allergy or something. I would be fine. That's what I told myself as I tasted the substance.

The moment it touched my tongue, I knew what it was. Well, I knew what it likely was anyway. It had a slight salty, minty flavor and brought me back to when I had a fever and Mom put powder medicine in my hot water. It was a pain reliever of some kind. Which didn't make sense . . . or maybe it did.

Last night, Lucy and I had analyzed Jaden's empty medicine bottle again and again, yet there was no clue as to what it was for, only that it was all gone. Which meant that maybe the missing medicine had somehow gotten ground up and put on our cookies. But I had no idea who could've done that, since we were all standing by our cookies the entire time—unless it was put on after. Or . . . during tasting? Either way, if it was a powder medicine—a pain reliever—how did that connect to Chef Remi?

Quickly, I nibbled each cookie, analyzing every flavor and ingredient I could. Nothing stood out at first. Also, Jaden's macarons were delicious—though the filling was a bit gritty. But then when I took a bite of Micah's cookie, I was immediately stumped. It tasted . . . medicinal in an entirely other way. I chewed carefully. Underneath the spices and ginger, there was something earthy. Some kind of savory herb that was a bit *off*. Didn't belong in a cookie. I stood there a few moments, tasting and thinking, waiting for a reaction—though hopefully not one that would cause me to choke, collapse, and go comatose like Chef Remi.

Another few moments passed and nothing happened. I tried to figure out what Micah had put in there, but before I could, I heard Lucy's voice loudly through the swing doors.

"Good morning, Chef Polly! . . . Oh, Laila? She went to the bathroom. She'll be back any second."

That was my cue. I scuttled back to the cafeteria in time to join the others without looking too suspicious. They were all turned in the direction of Chef Polly, so I grabbed a plate and put food on it, not caring what I picked.

Chef Polly was positively beaming with the attention she was getting, especially Lucy's, when she raised both arms. "Good morning! I'm so glad to see you all in good spirits. Now please take a seat. It's time to talk about our final challenges!" She waited for us to sit at our tables before continuing. "Now that y'all got a chance to grab a plate full of fabulous pastries made by Chef Noah, we can tell you what's in store for today."

Chef Noah sidled up to Polly, wearing a very crisp, very expensive chambray set of chef's whites embossed with his name. As if this had been hanging around his closet waiting for a chance to be worn after Chef Remi was out of the picture.

Like Polly, he seemed to be bouncing with excitement.

"First, we've been told that by the late afternoon, the roads outside should be clear enough for your rides home to come collect you. Isn't that great?"

I took a long breath and let it loose in relief. We could go home. We could see our families. We wouldn't be trapped in a school with a wannabe murderer. A murderer we hadn't uncovered. Still, something was very wrong here at Sunderland, and my little adventure to the cafeteria refrigerator hadn't changed that feeling.

"Second, we're going to flip the script a bit today. Your first challenge is going to be hard and very technical. We want desserts with the shape and size and appearance of a cookie, but not a cookie. Pies, cakes, puff pastry—you name it. Deceive us! Wow us. Don't disappoint us." Noah's eyes seemed to bore into mine when he said that last thing, and I felt hot around the collar of my shirt. Why did he say that and look at me? I thought Noah liked me. Wait . . . did he see me? No. But maybe?

I was so busy worrying about that prospect that when I glanced over at Jaden, his signature sneer almost brought me comfort.

Chef Polly cut in. "We're so proud of how far you've all made it and are inspired by your talent and flavors. We know you can do this! So eat up, prepare yourself, because today you'll find out who will win the Golden Cookie." She gave me a wink as if to make up for Noah's snub.

Then the two left us and a silence fell over the room.

"What did you find out?" Lucy asked, nibbling her oversize pain au chocolat. "Any clues?"

I shook my head and plucked a savory Danish off my plate. I needed something substantial after eating bits of cookies first thing in the morning. "Someone tampered with the cookies, but there wasn't poison. It's hard to explain."

The Danish crackled in my hand and I glanced down to marvel at the flaky, crisp crust before taking a big bite. Flavors exploded in my mouth again. Salty, buttery, cheesy—Parmesan with a touch of Gruyère and a hint of sweetness and . . . that same sharp citrus pesto that was in the sandwiches yesterday. Huh. I took another bite. The pesto worked much better in fresh pastries. It had a very memorable flavor to me, at least, though there wasn't much of it there. A taste enhancer. A signature taste enhancer.

Suddenly, I knew that Chef Noah had made the sandwiches from yesterday. He must've made them on day one. And then he made these this morning. But then why did he get pizza that day? What could that mean?

Lucy drummed her fingers against the edge of the table. "What are you going to do now?"

Oh, right. The competition. I polished off the Danish and gathered my thoughts. "I'm going to do my take on mini pecan pies for one, and for the second, vanilla sheet cake drizzled with hot caramel and then blowtorched till it's—"

"No, I mean, what are you going to do about the"—she lowered her voice—"almost murder? The way I see it, there are four suspects we haven't ruled out yet. Jaden, Micah, Chef Polly, *and* Chef Noah. And the cookies didn't lead anywhere new."

"They did." I sighed and leaned closer, my gaze darting across the room. "I think Micah might be involved, there was something . . . *off* in his cookie. I'll keep an eye on him while you break into the security office and find out who—"

Chef Polly suddenly stood beside our table, and the color drained from Lucy's face. My cheeks heated. Did she hear? Oh no. If she did hear, she didn't show it. Her charm bracelet jingled as she put a hand on Lucy's shoulder. "Lucy, I know you're writing an article about this weekend and hoping to submit it to the Sunderland scholarship committee—if I have that right?"

Lucy nodded slowly, her eyes wide. Her leg jiggled nervously and stamped beneath the table. She set the pastry down on the plate, her hands shaking slightly.

"Good! I was wondering if we could have a chat. I think I've got something exclusive to share with you that could be just the thing you need for an article. Mind following me to the kitchen?"

"Um . . . okay," Lucy said, her eyes meeting mine.

"I'll come with you," I offered, standing up.

"No, no, no need, honey." Chef Polly waved an authoritative hand in my direction. "Finish your breakfast with the other competitors and rest as long as you can. Lucy and I will be peachy, just the two of us, right?"

"Yup. Peachy," Lucy replied unconvincingly. She stood up, and before I could say anything else, Polly and Lucy left the cafeteria.

My heart pounded in my ears as I watched them turn a corner and disappear down the hallway. Lucy was in trouble. I didn't bother with my pastries or Jaden, who was still looking in my direction, probably to start a fight or whatever. No, I bolted to my feet and chased after them.

But when I got to the kitchen arena, they weren't there.

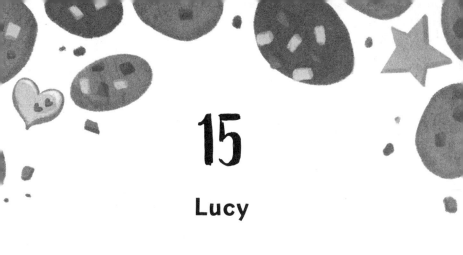

15

Lucy

I NODDED ALONG, pretending to pay attention to Chef Polly's story about guest hosting some morning show with a pushy doctor and too-smiley lawyer. But in reality, I was making note of every sign we passed by, every closed door. We started out heading toward the kitchen arena but then made a left instead of a right. For the past five minutes, we'd been moving away from where everyone else was. Away from where anyone could help me if anything went wrong.

With the storm passing, the lights had stopped flickering, but that didn't keep the whole building from feeling creepy. The classrooms we passed were dark. Our own faces reflected on the spotless windows as we strolled by, making it look like ghosts were flitting behind the doors. I shuddered.

"Well, don't you agree?" Chef Polly asked, her voice a

little higher. She must've asked a question and was repeating it.

I gulped. I didn't have any idea what that question was because I'd been taking a mental picture of the locked-up science lab we'd just passed. And planning the easiest escape route back to the others, because it was possible I was alone with a wannabe murderer. Who knew I was investigating.

I reached for a way to answer her without tipping her off to my nervousness. "I . . . um . . . who wouldn't agree?"

Chef Polly humphed in response, which was good, I guess? She at least didn't notice or point out that I wasn't listening.

"Anyway, that woman was the rudest makeup artist I've ever met," she continued. "You know what my ma used to call prickly people like that? Ones who never seemed to have a 'right side of the bed' to get up from?" She peered down at me, a glint in her smiling eyes. "Porcupines."

We both laughed, and it cut the uneasiness from the missed question and rambling path around the school. We turned a corner, and we strolled by a "Suggested Summer Reading" bulletin board I swore we'd walked by earlier.

"That Chef Remi, Ma would call him a porcupine too," Polly said, before quickly adding, "God rest his poor soul."

"He's still alive," I blurted unexpectedly, even to myself. Just the mention of Chef Remi almost made me trip over my own feet. I caught myself before I fell too far, but Chef Polly raised a sharp eyebrow at me.

"Yes, yes, my mistake," she said softly. "I'm simply so distraught over everything."

Then her lips pursed ever so slightly, and being the subject of her undivided attention suddenly sent a chill down my spine.

So I did what I do anytime I feel awkward: I reached for my phone.

The time on the lock screen shone out at me. I realized we were due back at the kitchen arena soon, so either I needed to get some answers or, well, she needed to hurry up and try to off me. I hoped for the first option. I didn't have my trusty wooden spoon with me.

But before I gathered the courage to tackle the tough subject of Chef Remi, Polly's face curved into her bright made-for-television smile at the sight of my phone. She clasped her hands together and stopped walking. "Finally! I was wondering when you were going to start taking notes. Here I was dropping these hints about my new show, and you didn't seem interested."

I paused next to her. "New show?" Was that what she separated me from the others for? Not to kill me, but to actually give me exclusive details about her work for my writing?

I had to admit, I wasn't expecting that. With all the

shady happenings and cutthroat competition, I'd forgotten that sometimes people just do exactly what they say they're going to do.

Polly chuckled, though I noticed a hint of impatience in it. "Why, yes, dear. Why do you think I was complaining about that porcupine of a set designer? You were supposed to ask me, 'Chef Polly, however will you handle that sticky situation?'"

She paused then, long enough that the awkwardness made me look at my phone again. Then I realized what she wanted. "Oh, um, Chef Polly, however will you handle that sticky situation?"

She winked at me. "Thought you'd never ask. I simply thanked the set designer for her hard work on my old show, then made a point to not have her join me on my new venture. I want a supportive staff, after all. The audience can tell when there's friction on the set, and I want only joy, joy, joy on *Chef Polly and Puppetfriends*!"

A laugh escaped me before I could stop it, and I covered it with a cough. "Puppets? And you?" The thought of Chef Polly on *Sesame Street* was hard not to keep laughing at. I barely managed to hide my smile by scratching some phantom itch on my nose.

"Yes, we'll be making tasty, nutritious meals that kids like you can follow along with. Wouldn't it be lovely to mention in your article how delightful and entertaining I am? And how wonderful I am with the little ones?"

"I guess so. But you know I just write for the school paper, right?" And I was definitely not going to use the phrase *little ones*.

Her TV smile strained. "Of course, but you're also submitting your portfolio to the Sunderland scholarship committee and administrators. Your application coach, Tonya, is an old country club friend of mine. She said you were looking for something to jazz up your portfolio. And, between you and me, these Sunderland committees are chock-full of wealthy investors, like pecans in a praline. You and I can help each other here with that writing sample, you see?"

The light bulb clicked in my head. She wanted me to write about her only so she could get people to fund her puppet cooking show. Or cooking puppet show. Whatever.

This whole conversation, porcupines and all, had nothing to do with Chef Remi.

Which led to another realization: Chef Polly wouldn't have been the one to mess with the cameras, then. If she was trying to get the attention of investors, she would've wanted all the footage of her being extra-nice to us broadcast as widely as possible. She was probably counting on the Sunderland board checking out the live feed, if only it had been operating glitch-free. Maybe it was why she'd been so desperate for her phone to work, so she could see if her performance was winning over investors.

Chef Polly didn't turn the cameras off. So who did?

I gulped, too aware of her staring at me. I couldn't write the article she wanted, not when there was a much bigger story about a potential murderer on the loose. I had to craft the perfect writing sample and, more important, prove to everyone—and myself—that I had the chops to do the hard-hitting journalistic work needed to pull off a piece like this. Chef Polly was not going to be pleased about that, and even though I hadn't known her that long, the thought made me pause.

I began with a question that hopefully wouldn't rile her too much. "So, um, you mentioned Chef Remi and how you thought he was 'prickly.'"

Chef Polly sniffed. "Must we really talk about him? I'm offering you a lovely topic to write on instead."

My courage flagged, but I pressed on. Her technological abilities—or lack of them—knocked her a bunch of rungs down on the suspect list, but I needed more information. "I—I do want to talk about him." I gulped. "How long have you known Chef Remi? And how would you describe your relationship with him?"

"Relationship," she practically spit. "Actually, fun fact:

one of the puppets on my show is modeled after him! Has the same snooty airs and everything. I—"

"Um, sorry, Chef Polly." I forced my voice louder, with a confidence that I hoped she didn't realize was fake, but I still had trouble holding eye contact. "This is great and all, but I don't think it's going to make it into my article."

She angled her head, and her dangly pearl earrings swayed. "May I ask why not, honey?"

I braced myself for her rage. But I needed something, anything, to help me figure out who tried to hurt Chef Remi, and playing it safe wasn't cutting it: I had to ruffle feathers, even if it ruffled my own, to get to the heart of the story I wanted to tell. "Because my article's going to be about what happened during the Golden Cookie Competition . . . what happened to Chef Remi."

Her pitying laughter rang down the empty hallway. "That might not be as compelling a piece as you think. Nothing *happened* to Chef Remi that he didn't do to himself. You heard what the doctors said about his heart issue, natural causes and all that."

Something about her tone reminded me of that jerk editor in chief Peter, the way he always found a way to belittle the assignments he gave me himself.

Was she covering up the foul play or did she actually

believe that nothing was amiss? She was so skilled in her perfect for-the-TV-camera persona that I couldn't tell, even with my eye for poker-face changes. I tried to find the courage that I'd have if Laila were standing next to me. "Right. It *looks* natural, but is it really? There are a lot of people here who hate Chef Remi."

"But hating the man is different than trying to kill him." She blew a breath out of her nose, her nostrils flaring. "No, honey, it's best you find another topic. Poking and prodding around on this nonsense will make a lot of people upset. Like that nice Principal Winters, don't you think?"

Her question was a punch in the gut. She was right. I hadn't considered that angle much because I was so focused on clearing Laila's name. An article about an attempted murder at the school was bound to upset Sunderland administrators. There wasn't any overlap between the admissions staff and the Ariella Wilborn Journalism Scholarship committee as far as I knew. I had already been admitted into the school. They couldn't revoke my admission, could they? Either way, it would take all my skill to craft a balanced, non-future-ruining portrayal of events. I didn't want to start the school year with enemies, if I was able to attend Sunderland at all.

I was faced with a big decision: Take the easier path of puppets and fluff that would keep everyone happy? Or forge ahead on the more hazardous path by investigating what happened to Chef Remi, upsetting any school administrators who wanted to keep the story quiet—not to mention angering that potential murderer?

I thought then of Laila and the whole Golden Cookie Competition: the reason we were here. She hadn't taken the easier path in any of the rounds. She'd challenged herself at every turn, even if she risked failure (and actually did fail, like with the BlenderFaceLucy cookie). But that hadn't stopped her. In fact, it made her one of the top competitors here.

And that was where I needed to be: the top. I had to be bolder and ask the tough questions, no matter who it upset, in order to tell the story the way I needed to tell it.

That was what Laila would do. That was what my hero, Ariella Wilborn, would do.

So that was exactly what I, Lucy Flores, would do.

Or at least try to do.

I gulped.

I sure could have used a tall glass of milk, preferably with one of Laila's Italian hazelnut–orange cookies, to make this newfound courage go down easier.

"I—I'm going to stick to my article about what happened to Chef Remi," I squeaked out.

Chef Polly gave a long, drawn-out sigh. "How very, very disappointing."

I tried not to wince at her comment.

"You will anger a lot of the people at Sunderland with your wild-goose chase, young lady," she reminded me.

I raised my chin. "If that's the price of truth, I'll pay it."

Chef Polly humphed under her breath. "We should head back to the kitchen arena."

I'd done it: I'd stood up for myself and my work.

As we walked back, she prattled on about her next show, a new iciness in her tone about how it was my loss for not seizing this opportunity. The old me would've felt guilty about upsetting her and offered to write something small on her show, just to make her happy. But there wasn't any time for that, and I knew I needed to focus on finding the potential murderer. This courage to tell the story was welcome but new, like a stylish pair of shoes two sizes too big that my mom swore I'd grow into.

At the rate Chef Polly and I were wandering the campus, we would be with the others soon, with a few minutes before the start of this morning's round. That would hopefully be enough time to check in with Laila and tell her what I'd deduced about Chef Polly. Maybe Laila would've gotten some more important, useful info while I was out here, wasting time.

At least we were narrowing down our list of suspects.

This should've made me feel relieved. But now that I'd ruled out Chef Polly from our list, all I could think about was that Laila was in a room full of people, and one of those people wanted to off Chef Remi.

I picked up the pace.

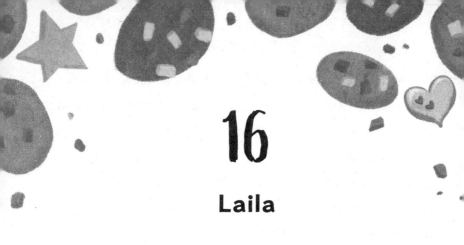

16

Laila

I TIED MY polka-dot apron strings, my eyes on the doors. Lucy still wasn't back, and while everyone was getting prepped, my heart was pounding in my ears. What if Chef Polly was the real villain and she'd kidnapped Lucy . . . or worse? Where could they have gone? What if she was telling her what she did to Chef Remi and explaining how Lucy was next, and this time she wouldn't make the mistake of letting her victim live? I dropped my arms. I needed to go search for her again. What if—

My thoughts were cut off when Chef Polly and Lucy strolled into the kitchen. Chef Polly looked slightly annoyed. Her smile was a little too thin, her cheeks stretched a little too tight. She stepped in front of the judges' table and clasped her hands together.

My gaze flicked to Lucy, and she shook her head, which I interpreted to mean either: Yes, Chef Polly's the would-be killer—don't go near her! Or: No, Chef Polly was innocent for reasons she'd tell me later. Being best friends for years meant we were able to read each other's expressions. Usually. Hopefully. I think? Either way, I was staying at my workstation and as far as I could from Chef Polly.

Chef Noah arrived, an oversize ring of keys jingling from a loop at his hip as he walked. His eyes were a bit glazed as if he were somewhere else while he smiled at us. Which got me wondering where he'd been since the breakfast announcement. He wasn't with Lucy or Polly, so where was he? What was he doing? What were those keys to? He was usually in the kitchen arena preparing for us, but the place was empty when I came here early to catch Chef Polly and Lucy.

Lucy perched on her usual kitchen stool. She grabbed her notebook and began scribbling on it. Meanwhile, Chef Polly waited for Chef Noah to stand beside her before she kicked off the competition.

"You all know the rules of the challenge. Happy baking!" She smiled again at us, then her eyes narrowed on Noah. There was a long look shared between the two. But I had no time to wonder why they were all being so weird. The competition was in full swing, and if I didn't win today, that would be it for me and Lucy at Sunderland. . . . And that made me sad, but also it didn't hurt my heart as much as I thought it would.

I ran to the walk-in refrigerator to grab the fancy French butter as fast as I could without causing a catastrophe in the process. My shoulder narrowly missed Jaden, and he turned sharply.

"Hey! Watch where you're going!"

Which was when I noticed his hands were shaking, and the color had leached from his face. He looked close to fainting. I slowed down and stepped beside his bench, taking in his hunched-over form and how slowly he moved.

"You don't look good," I said carefully, and when his gaze pierced mine angrily, I added, "Well, you never look good. But you look worse right now."

He sighed, and I braced for him to yell at me, tell me I was a cheater, or call me names as he usually did, but he didn't. He leaned into me. "I have a migraine, and my medicine is . . . I can't find it anywhere. Even my backup homeopathic tea mixture is gone."

The baggie from the walk-in. Tea, like I thought. And hmm . . . what if the powder on top of the cookies was his medicine? Something fishy was going on. "A migraine? That's a really bad headache, right?"

Jaden rolled his eyes, and this was the first time in forever he actually didn't say anything awful to me. Maybe he was nice only when he was feeling unwell. "Yes, a really bad headache."

Thoughts circulated around my brain. "Why don't you ask one of the judges if they have some . . . I don't know, aspirin or something?"

"Yeah, why don't I also tell them I want to lose right now?" His snark had a little less bite to it. When I pursed my lips, he shook his head. "If they know I'm not feeling well, they'll make me stop competing. And you'd love that, wouldn't you?"

"No." I stood tall and raised my chin. "I want to beat you fair and square. But didn't you tell them you had migraine issues before you started the competition? Wouldn't they want to help you? They have to offer accommodations or something, right?"

Jaden let a long breath whoosh through his teeth. "Yeah, Chef Remi knew and said I shouldn't be allowed to compete. Chef Noah talked him into letting me come if I used the tea mixture while in the kitchen. But now . . ."

"Now you need meds. Wait . . . my dad used to get those." I remembered him not being able to look at bright lights and how loud noises hurt him. He would've never baked in a hot kitchen with me if his head hurt. Jaden had to be suffering, and it explained why he needed to bend down yesterday. He wasn't well. "Hold on."

I sprang past the judges' table, where Polly and Noah were noticeably absent. It didn't matter. Lucy gave me a thumbs-up like a question, and I nodded before bolting over toward the drinks station. With a push of a button, hot water poured into a mug, and I slipped a bag of green tea into it. If there was anything I knew about green tea, it was that it was strong, had lots of caffeine, which helped headaches, and got bitter and yucky if it sat in the hot water too long. While that steeped, I soaked a hand towel in ice-cold water. After two minutes, I removed the tea bag and the freezing-cold cloth and brought them back to Jaden.

"Drink this as soon as it cools." I slid the tea onto his bench in front of him. As he gave me the weirdest expression, I hung the cold cloth around his neck. "It's not as good as medicine or your other homeopathic tea stuff, but . . . it should help."

Jaden exhaled slowly. "I had a migraine the first day. I told Chef Remi I needed my stronger meds, but he said I couldn't leave to go get my medicine in my room. I had a backup tea mixture in my pocket, which I ended up spilling in the walk-in. When I tried to tell the judges, Remi was being such a jerk about it. . . . Anyway, why are you helping me?"

I fought the urge to shrug and say something about how I didn't care or whatever. Instead my mouth blurted the one thing I never expected it would. "My dad got migraines all the time when he started chemotherapy. He used to drink coffee or green tea and put an ice pack on his head or a cold cloth. He . . . didn't always feel great, but he loved cooking and baking like you, and I don't know, it's not really fair." My tone sounded airy and weird, and tears prickled suddenly around my eyes. I sniffed. "Maybe it'll help you feel better. Besides, I told you I want to beat you fair and square." I smiled and tried to sound cool and competitive again. Jaden didn't seem to buy it.

"I know you didn't cheat." He touched his hand to my arm as I tried to back away.

"What?" My mind almost blanked. Of all the things I thought Jaden would say, it wasn't that.

"At the pie competition," Jaden added. "I overheard one of the judges talking about how your dad died? I don't know. I guess I figured she let you win because she felt bad. I shouldn't have blamed you. I'm—I always mess things up."

"I—she might've, I don't know. I didn't mean for it to happen." And with that, my shoulders sagged; the truth had lifted the burden. "I'm sorry."

"No, I'm sorry for the way I treated you. I tasted your pie after and it was better than mine. I just, I guess, wanted to blame you. This is all I have." He still clasped my arm, and there was a new expression on his face. Like . . . compassion. Who knew Jaden could be nice? Who knew he could say I did something better than him? "I spent so much time traveling the world with my dads, I never got a chance to make friends or . . . or learn to talk to kids my own age. I thought being mean would make it easier to win. That way I wouldn't, you know, feel like I'm losing friends I kinda . . . like and wish I could hang out with? My brother goes here so he can stay in one place while our dads shoot their documentaries. Now it's my turn and I don't want to travel anymore, and I don't want to mess anything else up. I want to earn my Sunderland spot."

That was the most Jaden had spoken to me, and the most honest he'd been, in the entire competition. Suddenly, I didn't hate him so much anymore. I guessed, maybe, I would feel the same way—I just wouldn't be so mean about it.

And then something weird happened. I smiled at Jaden. "I hope you feel better. And if you win, I hope you know, you deserve it. You're really good."

"So are you." He took a sip of tea before responding, and his face relaxed a little. "And I don't need to taste the cookies to know that you didn't try to kill Chef Remi. I'm sorry for saying it . . . for everything."

My cheeks heated as I nodded, and then I took off to

the walk-in, where there wasn't enough of the fancy butter anymore. Helping Jaden set me back, but . . . I took a deep breath. I wouldn't have done anything differently.

I took the rest of the regular butter and hoped it was all going to work out.

When I returned to my bench, Noah and Polly were back at the judges' table, their faces flushed pink, and Polly was glaring at her phone as if begging it to ring. Lucy was eyeing them closely and I was severely behind on my pastry cookie concoctions.

Right. Baking. Baking for a place at prestigious, expensive Sunderland. Easy. No pressure. First, I prepared my thin vanilla sponge. It was a bit thinner than I normally made, but then, it was supposed to look like a cookie. I slid the sheet pan into the oven and then began my pie crust, moving fast but carefully. I set that in the freezer, which was stuffed full of everyone's dough and fillings already. The clock was ticking, and while I was panicking about how I was going to get my pecan pies done on time, Chef Polly's voice pierced the room.

"What do you mean, Noah?" she exclaimed, hands on her hips. "When were you going to tell me?"

"Now, Polly, don't make a scene, the children shouldn't be hearing this." He threw his arms out, gesturing to us. Across the room, I noticed Micah staring, mouth open.

Same with Maeve, Philippa, and Jaden. Lucy was frantically scribbling in her notebook. Knowing her, she must've heard everything and more.

"They should know!" she shrieked as she turned our way. "This is trouble! Can you imagine the press and how this is going to look?"

"What happened, Chef Polly?" Lucy asked. Her voice trembled, like she was forcing herself to be brave.

"Someone"—Polly looked Lucy directly in the eyes—"called the police on the landline phone this morning and told them that they have proof that someone in this kitchen tried to . . . to *kill* Chef Remi!"

On the last word, her voice cracked and her body seemed close to crumbling. Lucy leapt up to help Polly into her judges' table seat before she could faint, although Polly seemed to think the caller was Lucy. The police knew it was foul play, but if someone had proof—actual proof—connecting one of us to it . . .

Polly fanned herself with her hand. "Who would've . . . I don't—" She slumped farther. "And now the doctors are saying they think it was something to do with his medicine and if they don't find out what he took, he might—"

"Enough," Noah's voice boomed through the kitchen. "We'll talk about this later. This doesn't concern you all.

Competitors, I'll give you ten extra minutes on your challenges today as Chef Polly comes to her senses. Chef Remi is very much alive yet comatose. He'll be okay. There's nothing to worry about." Noah smiled as if to reassure us and then escorted a trembling Polly out of the room. I tilted my head in Lucy's direction.

She knew what I was thinking. *Follow them.*

Lucy snuck after the chefs as the rest of us went about our cooking.

I knew I wasn't the only one having difficulty focusing. Someone in this room called the police and said what happened to Chef Remi wasn't an accident. It couldn't have been me, since I hadn't used the phone, or Lucy, who hadn't had the time to call anyone either. It couldn't be Polly: she was clearly and very overwhelmingly surprised, and she and Lucy were on that walk together before the round started.

That meant one of my fellow competitors called the police because they saw something suspicious, or . . . they knew because they were the one who tried to murder him and they had a plan to frame someone else.

Frame someone like me, since it was my cookies Remi was eating when he choked and collapsed. There was white powder on the cookies in the walk-in. Micah's cookies were off too.

Maybe it was Micah? I swallowed my growing worries. And then a thought struck me. "Philippa, Maeve, on our first day, did you see Jaden's medicine in the walk-in?"

They both stopped working and glanced at each other, and Jaden looked up.

Maeve answered first. "I thought I saw a medicine bottle behind the butter. I didn't know who it belonged to though."

"Yeah, why does this matter?" Philippa's face was pinched, and she slammed her sheet pan down on the table. "If you haven't noticed, we are competing and—"

"Was the medicine bottle full?" I interjected.

"I don't know," Maeve said, her brow furrowed. "I didn't check. Sorry."

"How did it get in there? I left it in my room." Jaden scratched his head.

But I didn't have an answer—all I could do was think about what it meant. The person who tried to kill Chef Remi knew about Jaden's medicine. That person took the medicine before round two began, maybe even before round one. Which meant . . . someone could have switched out Chef Remi's pills with Jaden's, and that kind of science experiment could be deadly.

I glanced over at Micah, who kept his head down as he

worked. Micah shared a room with Jaden. . . . His cookies didn't taste right. He'd hinted at everyone else's connection to Chef Remi but his own.

What would he do if he knew I suspected him? Would he shut me up like he did Chef Remi?

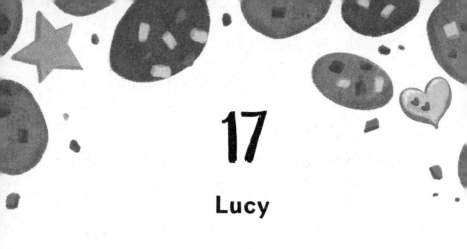

17

Lucy

THE KITCHEN ARENA doors actually smacked me on the butt on the way out. As if they were saying, "Hurry up, slowpoke!"

Not that I needed the reminder. I jumped out of my chair to follow Chef Polly and Chef Noah as they stepped out, and they were already around the corner. Who knew these old people could move so fast?

I realized then that, in my rush, I left my phone, pen, wooden spoon, everything back in the kitchen. I couldn't go back now, not without losing the chefs completely. Ariella Wilborn wouldn't let these suspicious-acting folks out of her sight. Neither would I.

I snaked from potted plant to lounge chair to trash can, prepared to hide at a microsecond's notice. Keeping up with these speed-walking chefs—Polly really must be upset—was a challenge, but I was proud to admit I was doing a great job of it.

And the PE teacher had the audacity to give me a B minus. Psh.

Noah's voice echoed against the bare walls and reached me. "Take a deep inhale, Polly. The rain's stopped, if you need fresh air."

"I don't need fresh air, Noah. I need answers!" There was a breathlessness to the way she was talking, like she wanted all the oxygen in the school to fuel her walk-jogging and shrieking. "Wait." She suddenly stopped, and I curled behind a tall, black trash bin to stay out of sight. "The children! We must get back. Their safety!"

My mind flew to the competition manual sitting in our dorm room. Laila and I pored over it last night, trying to find any contact information or to compare it to what'd been happening. But communication with anyone other than through the landline—which, hello, of course the murderer was going to keep an extra eye on now—was still spotty, and every bit of the competition had actually followed the Golden Cookie rules to a tee.

Until now.

No one was allowed to leave the kitchen arena once the round started. Chef Noah made a huge deal about it the first day when Chef Polly wanted to step out for a few minutes.

But all of a sudden, both judges were out here? Did Noah drag Polly out here to get her alone?

"Safety is not an issue," Chef Noah said. "All this talk about Remi being murdered—almost murdered—is nonsense. The police are wrong. The children are in no danger. Sunderland has state-of-the-art security for everything."

His voice was as calm as it was in the kitchen arena, as if talking to kids and talking to the esteemed Chef Polly Rose were the same thing. It struck me then that he seemed much more concerned with trying to protect us, "the children," from Chef Polly's outburst than he was about the news that the doctors were rethinking what happened to his longtime boss. He was frantic when Chef Remi collapsed. What caused this change in him? Was it optimism that his boss was truly fine and recovering? Or guilt over hurting the chef in the first place?

Chef Polly blew out a breath. "Yes, I suppose you're right. The police will be able to check all the security records and confirm the doctors' report in no time. . . . What? What's the look for, Noah?"

For a moment, I was tempted to pop my head above the trash bin to see Noah's expression. That would've told me a lot about what was going through his mind. Unfortunately, it would've also revealed that I'd been eavesdropping and they'd end my investigation real quick. Chef Polly probably wouldn't even have had me write her puppet show piece after that.

"I don't know where they keep all those security records. The police will probably take forever trying to search the school or contact the administrators, and don't you think it's important we get these poor kids home as soon as possible?"

My eyebrow raised. Noah was hard to read. One moment he was offering me a seat with a great view of the competition, and the next he was snootily demanding everyone call him "Chef." And now he was back to caring about us?

I guessed when you worked so closely and for so long with a strong personality like Chef Remi, though, that bully behavior rubbed off on you. I was lucky that the person I spent the most time with was Laila. The most she had rubbed off on me was her courage and flour from her cookies.

"Let's get back to the kitchens, then," Chef Polly said. "We can call the board on the landline and ask about access."

This meant I had to get to the security room and use these newfound lockpicking skills before the chefs did. If someone here had the keys to unlock that stubborn door, they might enter and accidentally—or purposely—tamper with whatever evidence was in there before the investigators and I got a chance to dig in. I needed the hard, undeniable filmed proof to back up my story and my best friend's innocence.

Chef Noah mumbled something sounding like agreement, but I was too busy panicking to hear it. They were turning around and coming back this way.

And I was sitting right here between them and the kitchen arena.

The corner was too far away. There was no way I could slip around it fast enough.

What would Laila have done?

Her voice drifted through my head. *If you can't beat the cookie, become the cookie.*

I almost groaned aloud. What did that even mean?

Then something clicked. *If I can't hide behind the trash, become the trash.*

I curled myself up as small as possible and tugged the sleeves and hood of my sweatshirt down to cover every inch of exposed skin. I pulled the cloth over my knees, with the tips of my shoes barely sticking out. *Please let this attempt to resemble an inanimate sack of clothes work.*

The ground shook with each step the chefs took toward the kitchen. I held my breath as they passed me.

I stayed still for another few seconds after they turned the corner, just in case. My legs trembled as I uncurled and rose.

With the police on their way and the potential murderer

no doubt under pressure, it wasn't a safe time to head for the security room. And even if I ran there, who knew how long it would take for me to get the door open? The only other option was returning to the kitchen arena, so making up my mind on a direction was as easy as pie.

Or should I have said "as easy as cookies"?

I sighed to myself. I'd definitely been spending too much time with Laila if all her nonsensical baking sayings had melted into my brain like this.

I crept into the kitchen arena right as Chef Noah counted down the last few seconds of the round. The frenzy of the kitchen—his voice booming, plates and utensils smacking against each other, aprons swishing as competitors ran—covered the slight creak of the door as I nudged it open.

By the time he hit "Three, two, one! Step away from your workstations!" I'd crawled on my hands and knees back to my workstation, then popped up on my stool as if I'd just been rummaging through my backpack for something.

But if anyone took a closer look, they would've noticed the sweat on my forehead from the run here. And the sugar dotting my palms and pants from my time on the floor.

Suddenly, Chef Polly locked eyes with me. I fought the

urge to look away, because for all she knew, I had nothing to hide. I was here the whole time and not at all following them, right?

Then her face shifted into TV mode as she moved to stand next to Chef Noah. If Chef Noah was hard to read, Chef Polly was harder, with that perfect TV persona. It astonished me how she could switch her smiley, camera-ready disposition on and off like a light switch. Anyone else might have missed that icy glint in her eye, but not me. I could tell she was upset about these latest developments around what happened to Chef Remi. She was trying her best to hide it, probably for the sake of us, "the children!"

The two chefs strolled through the room, tasting the competitors' cookies. I wondered if anyone else noticed how stiff the chefs' movements were, how they were making an effort to stand on opposite ends of the workstations from each other.

I caught Laila's gaze then, as the chefs critiqued Micah's work. Typical Micah: he had played this challenge as safely as he could. He'd made a chocolate cake and decorated it to look like a chocolate chip cookie.

I was surprised Laila was able to tear her heart-eyes away from Micah the Mighty to look at me, but this time, I caught a cloud of something else in there. Maybe her crush was already fading. Then Laila tilted her head sharply at the chefs, as if to say, "What's going on there?"

So at least she saw something was off too. It was up to me to find out what those secrets were. Laila's job was to blow everyone away with her baking.

And she did not disappoint.

Despite her earlier sourness, Chef Polly actually giggled after taking a bite of Laila's work. "The way you caramelized this sugar on top! It's like biting into a spoonful of sinful crème brûlée." She patted a beaming Laila on the shoulder. "Well done, honey."

Chef Noah's face stayed still as he chewed. "The custard in these mini pecan pies is a little runny for my tastes, but the flavor is there."

Everyone else in the room made a face when Noah dared to call Laila's mini pecan pies runny. From here, those cookie-looking pecan pies appeared perfect. After this round ended, I was going to shovel the rest of that batch in my mouth to prove the point.

Chef Noah and Chef Polly reached Jaden's workstation last. Despite the "step back from your workstation" instruction, Jaden's hand was splayed on the countertop, like he was holding himself up.

Polly set down her sample after taking a bite. "This matcha sponge is wonderful. But you're looking a little—ill. Everything all right, young man?"

Come to think of it, Jaden did look worse than usual. He was pale again, and his jaw was tight.

I didn't think anything else could surprise me this weekend, but Jaden's next words did.

"No, actually. I've got a migraine, and the only reason I was able to bake at all is because Laila helped me handle the pain."

Laila being back to her usual helpful self wasn't a surprise at all, but Jaden acting nice about it made my jaw drop. One look at Laila, who was actually smiling at him—yes, the one who accused her of trying to murder Chef Remi with her cookies—confirmed it. Something must've gone down while I was sneaking up on Polly and Noah.

Meanwhile, the chefs had drawn aside to discuss the desserts. The quick hand movements, the rapid head shakes, the rolling of their eyes—there was definitely a tension that wasn't there in previous rounds.

Chef Polly spun on her kitten heels while Chef Noah was midsentence. "We have a winner!"

Chef Noah's eyes flared with anger for a microsecond. I don't think anyone else caught it—I was probably the only one in the room focused on clues and tells rather than the upcoming announcement—but it was clear enough that I made a mental note to write it down in my notebook later.

Whatever Chef Polly was about to say, Chef Noah might not have agreed with. But as backup judge, he might not have felt ready to challenge her.

"Or should I say, winners?" Chef Polly's smile widened. "In the spirit of the Golden Cookie, we encourage and reward good behavior. So I'm pleased to announce the joint winners are Jaden and Laila!"

I was up on my feet clapping even as my brain raced a mile a minute. With Jaden and Laila as cowinners and Chef Remi's near death resulting in no one winning round two, this meant Laila's victory wasn't as secure as we'd hoped. If Jaden won the last round, there could be a tie between him and Laila. But who got that Sunderland admission if that happened?

A truce may have settled between Laila and our once enemy Jaden, but the air in Sunderland Academy still felt too heavy, like it was carrying too many secrets. The storm was passing, sunlight starting to peek through the gray. The police and our parents would be here in a matter of hours. We'd be whisked back home, cutting off our ability to get the answers we needed for ourselves and for Laila's reputation. That meant this was Laila's and my last chance to crack this case ourselves, but our list of suspects seemed to shift by the minute.

We had one more round of the Golden Cookie Competition to go.

And as we'd seen, anything could happen in one round: a cracked egg, a burned cookie, a suspicious accident. It looked like Laila and I might both be running short on time to chase our dreams.

18

Laila

WHEN WE BROKE for lunch, Philippa and Maeve shuffled past me without a look or hello, Micah shook his head at me, and Jaden smiled shakily before wandering off. I caught up with Lucy as we walked toward the cafeteria. The idea of eating right then made me a little sick to my stomach. I should be over the moon: I was one of the winners. Jaden and I were nearly tied for the spot at Sunderland. It was so close to being over.

But I didn't feel excited. I was worried about Lucy and about a potential murderer in our midst. I was worried about losing too, yet more than that, there was a big mystery at the center of this weekend, and I still hadn't unraveled it. My prime suspect had shifted from my enemy, Jaden, to my crush, Micah the Mighty. He'd told me everything I wanted to hear. He'd cast my suspicions elsewhere, was kind, friendly . . . helped me interrogate Jaden. He was the perfect new friend, maybe too perfect.

I was both disappointed and terrified. And worse, I had no idea how to get him to talk. I had no leverage.

Meanwhile, Lucy waited until everyone was far down the hall before she spilled everything. Her voice was a soft whisper, and she was certain of two things: one, Chef Noah was hiding something; and two, Chef Polly was farther down on the suspect list because her new TV show had her on her best behavior.

In the cafeteria, we plonked onto our seats at a table farthest away from everyone else. Today, there were sandwiches . . . again. They looked like ham, pesto, turkey, and mozzarella. They were slightly limp but delicious, if only my stomach weren't in knots. Philippa took the mozzarella one, Maeve the ham, and Micah the turkey, while Jaden was probably back in his room scrounging for something to help his migraine. I didn't have to wonder who made the food this time. I knew it was Chef Noah because of that signature pesto I could smell across the room.

After watching everyone pick at their cold sandwiches, I began to wonder something else entirely.

"The campus was closed down and flooded the entire weekend, right?" I asked Lucy as she eyed the table of sandwiches and her face turned a bit green.

She nodded. "That's why no one could come in, no one could go out. The roads."

I pursed my lips. "Remember there was pizza on day one?"

"That was before the storm," Lucy said slowly. "Chef Noah went to a pharmacy off campus to pick up Chef Remi's prescription early in the day. He must've gotten the pizza too, or it was delivered."

Lucy's brow furrowed then, like she saw it too: there was something weird about all of this, but I couldn't quite put my finger on what exactly. The questions came one after another: Were the roads really that flooded? Why did we have old sandwiches? Why were both Noah and Polly being weird? I had no answers, though. It seemed like Jaden's medicine was the biggest clue, but I couldn't figure out who took it.

When Micah reached for another sandwich, I called out to stop him. "Hey, save one for Jaden. He's probably starving while looking for medicine." Micah backed off, grabbing a brown-spotted banana instead, then seated himself back next to his potted plant.

Lucy tilted her head at me. "Medicine?"

"Jaden has migraines, pretty bad ones like . . . my dad did. He said Remi didn't want him in the competition but Noah talked him into it."

"That's not fair, and I'm pretty sure it's illegal to not let someone compete because they have an illness. I'm glad Jaden was allowed to come, although . . ." Lucy trailed off, nibbling her lip. "He's missing his medicine?" She suddenly bent over to dig through her bag. With a huff, she set her phone on the table. "Still no reception. Ugh. I just want to look something up."

I was about to ask Lucy if she thought there was something fishy about the reception, cameras, and roads all being nonfunctional—as if someone wanted them to be—and what she was going to look up, but then Philippa's voice pierced the room. She was on edge and seemed weirdly furious.

"I bet it was you." She pointed a finger at Lucy. "You were missing two days in a row. I thought we could trust you, but you're up to something, and all of us deserve to know what you were doing. I don't buy that you weren't feeling well."

Immediately I jumped to my feet, hands on my hips, head held high. "Lucy didn't try to kill Chef Remi! You've lost your marbles!"

Philippa shook her head. "No, I'm saying Lucy disappeared throughout the competition and she called the police to say that she had proof that someone tried to murder Chef Remi. Now we're all under suspicion, including our families. Do you have any idea how all of this will look? My mom and dad—we didn't—*I* didn't—"

Lucy stood up too, surprising me. She never got into confrontations if she didn't have to. That's what I was for, that was my job. But she didn't need me. "I didn't call the police. Neither did Laila. It must've been one of you."

Maeve pushed away from the table. "Why would any of us do that? Everyone said it was his heart, didn't they? We'd have no reason to report anything. It doesn't make any sense. Someone's trying to sabotage this competition and our families."

"And someone tried to commit murder," Micah said so quietly we almost didn't hear him.

We all turned slowly to Micah as Jaden stalked into the room. "What's going on?"

Philippa's voice got louder. "Maybe it was you and Laila, then! You played us all with your constant bickering and finger-pointing, but you're actually a team, aren't you? You're probably dating, too."

Jaden's face paled like he had one of his migraines again. "What?"

Even Maeve nodded. "After two days of fighting, suddenly you're acting like best friends. . . . It's suspicious is all we're saying."

I was totally speechless. Suspicious? Why would they think that? And then I realized that was exactly what Lucy and I had thought about Maeve and Philippa. Only they *were* dating. My mind flooded with a lot of things at once. Jaden and me? Impassable roads.

"I'm not . . . We're not . . ."

Jaden laughed, slapping his hand down on a table at the same time. "Me dating Laila? Are you serious?" I crossed my arms. What was wrong with dating me? I wasn't the worst. In fact, I was actually pretty cool. And I was about to say as much when Jaden cut in again. "When I came here, I didn't like Laila and Lucy. I didn't like any of you. I want to . . . I mean, I want to like you all, even you, Philippa, but especially Laila—"

My face suddenly felt hot and I looked at Lucy, whose eyebrows were nearly up to her hairline.

"They aren't dating. Laila's just a nice person." Micah's voice had a surprising edge to it as he stood up. Unlike the rest of us, he had no accusations to hurl. Which made me tense.

"Look, I get that everyone has been keeping secrets and everyone's angry." I tried to sound like I was calming the room down, like I was in control. I hoped it worked. "Maybe we would—we should—tell our truth? Micah, what about you? Are there secrets *you're* keeping?"

Micah's eyebrows rose. "*What?*"

"Something was wrong with your cookies," I blurted. "They didn't taste right."

Lucy piped up, "You didn't like Chef Remi. . . ."

"I can't believe this!" Micah shook his head, but the corner of his lip twitched. He was hiding something. Lucy and I were right. "No one liked Chef Remi."

"You had a history, you and your family," Lucy needled him in a steady voice. "Like everyone else's family here. A fact you didn't want us to know, which is why you pointed at everyone else."

Philippa slid a hand on her hip right as Maeve gasped. Meanwhile, Jaden took a sandwich and a seat at our table and wolfed it down while watching everything unfold. It was nice to not have him accusing me for once.

"I don't owe any of you an explanation or the truth." Micah looked angry, his voice a smidgen below a yell. "If I said I didn't do it, I didn't do it. You can believe me or not."

Philippa huffed. "You told Lucy and Laila all about our families and connections to Chef Remi, and don't think you should have to tell them yours?"

"Yeah," Maeve said with sudden anger we hadn't seen in her before. "You *do* owe us an explanation."

"Agreed." Jaden took another sandwich from the pile we'd basically abandoned. "This 'sensitive, sporty guy with a pet plant' thing you have going is as fake as white chocolate."

"Look," I said, trying to smooth over Jaden's edgy accusation. "No one wants you to feel uncomfortable. But—" I stepped closer to him, met his gaze. "I think we need to know."

"Fine." Micah exhaled slowly. "It's true that Chef Remi nearly caused us to go bankrupt. When he started getting into Korean cuisine, my parents called him out for cultural appropriation. It was like . . . he wasn't only making Korean food, he was saying how much better he made it than Korean people—it was really messed up. He didn't take their criticism well, and then posted a rambling bad review of the restaurant on social media. Anyway, yeah, my parents hate him for it, but we have a four-point-seven rating online and people love it."

Lucy and I exchanged a glance. "Uh . . . ?"

Micah shook his head. "All of that happened when I was six and the restaurant was starting out. Mom and Dad had moved over from Korea with all their savings. My older sisters had to clean and babysit me. Mom and Dad had to take out a second mortgage. It was bad. For a while. We're good now. I wouldn't even know how to . . . try to murder someone?" He gave his signature shrug. "So, yeah, my story's like the rest of theirs." He nodded in the direction of Philippa and Jaden. "Only mine has a happy ending."

I wasn't sure he cared about much before, but I could tell then that I was wrong. I had to press on. "Your cookies—"

Micah held up a hand. "I added my homegrown sage to the freshly grated ginger in my snap cookies and the flavors didn't mesh well. They seemed to be fighting each other. It tasted weird. That's all."

Philippa scoffed. "You and your potted plant. How do we know you didn't do something else? How do we know—"

"Exactly! Mr. Muscles over here is telling us exactly what we want to hear." Jaden stood up, though he looked a bit wobbly on his feet. "That doesn't explain why you've been baking like a newbie. We all know you're talented, so why were you making weird, boring mistakes?"

"First of all—" Micah stood taller and crept toward Jaden, leaving me in the middle. "I work out and play sports because if I can't do baking, I have nothing else. I suck at school. I hate math. But plants, sports, food—I can do those. I can work with my hands. And secondly . . ." His voice lost its anger and his eyes fell to the floor. "Secondly, I made weird mistakes because I was trying to impress someone. Only . . . I didn't know how."

"*Pffft*," Jaden said. "Who, Chef Remi? Weren't we all."

"Laila. I was trying to impress Laila." Micah's face turned a deep shade of red as thoughts momentarily fled my mind. "I saw her at a competition once. I don't think she saw me. She was . . . just so cool. And then I got here and she was nice to me and I didn't know what to do. And I wanted to make something extraordinary, bursting with new and unique flavors, but I kept messing up and went back to the basics. Anyway . . ." Micah cleared his throat; even his ears were a little red as he looked up at Jaden and everyone else but me. "Anyway, I'm innocent, like I think the rest of you are." He scrubbed a hand over his mouth before continuing. "Something's wrong with this competition, and it has been from the very beginning. Which is why I called the police. Don't you all see that?"

There was a collective gasp. Lucy's lips pinched while she tapped her pen on the notebook and glanced up at me quickly with an expression that said, "We are going to talk about this later." And yeah, we totally were! Micah was trying to impress me?! Me, Laila? Still, Lucy and I needed to stay on task. "Do you mean as in how you four, specifically, were picked to compete, when all of you have ties to Chef Remi and a motive?"

"Yeah," Maeve said before cringing at Philippa's expression. "She's right, though."

"I wasn't supposed to be here; Chef Noah told me that the first day," I added, though I was reeling from what Micah had said. No, I couldn't think about that. Something serious and bad had happened, and we needed to focus on that. Micah the Mighty would have to wait. "But all of you were."

They stood there, shifting on their feet. Even Jaden hung his head low.

"You all knew that and so did your parents, right? Your parents are friends—brought together by their shared hatred of Chef Remi." Lucy's voice cut through the uncomfortable silence. "That's why they tried to blame Laila. Why they didn't put up too much of a fuss about the stream not working. They thought one of you might've done it and they were protecting you."

I took Lucy's lead and held my head high. It was good to know there was a reason everyone blamed me and not because of how I looked. Though it didn't make me feel too much better either. "Does anyone know what happened to the cameras?"

"It wasn't me." Jaden's head tilted to the side. "I was wondering about that. If my dads weren't so busy, I had planned on asking them about whether the live stream ever came back up. They're always working, but at least they could pop onto the stream to see me."

"I didn't do it either," Philippa said sheepishly. "When I finally got through on the landline, I asked my mom and she said it wasn't working at all. She thinks it's the storm. Though the storm's not so bad back home."

"That's what my dad said this morning," Maeve said. "He said he watched the news, and while there's a typical summer storm in the area with some flooding, there are no outages. Maybe Sunderland's electricity and stuff is old. I didn't know they weren't working till the Zoom call."

And that's when that thing I was thinking about earlier beamed into my brain like a flashlight. "What if the streets are fine? What if it's a regular storm and everything is happening because someone planned it?"

"The weather?" Philippa rolled her eyes. "How would someone plan all of that?"

"I think you and Lucy are right." Micah stood tall and mighty. "When I spoke to my family, they'd heard from Chef Polly that Chef Remi had a heart attack. She said there wasn't foul play and that it was natural, because of his heart issues—"

"I saw him take his medicine," Lucy cut in. "Right in front of me."

Maeve gasped. "He did? Why didn't you say anything before?"

"Yeah," Philippa interjected. "If you knew Chef Remi took his meds, how come you didn't tell everyone when we thought that was the reason he's . . . you know, in a coma. You knew the whole time there was a potential murderer, and you didn't think to share it with the rest of us?"

"We didn't know who to trust," I interrupted, standing close to Lucy. "None of you told us you knew Chef Remi before the competition. You've all been keeping secrets."

Philippa huffed and Maeve shrank a little. Jaden kept quiet.

"We all know now that something's off." Micah threw up his hands, as if to tell us all to calm down. "I haven't been able to put everything together, but I swear . . . I saw something the first day we were here. Someone went into our—"

Micah was cut off by Chef Noah clapping his hands at the cafeteria entrance. Everyone jumped.

Chef Noah eyed us. "My, you are a close bunch! Are you kids coming to compete or do you want to chitchat some more? You know what's at stake, right? Admission and a full ride to Sunderland for four years. One challenge stands in your way! This is the moment you've all been working toward, the moment you've all been waiting for!"

He paused until we put a little excitement in our expressions before he smiled, though it didn't quite reach his eyes. "I'm sorry to say that Chef Polly isn't feeling well, so she's going to be sitting this one out. Not to worry, she'll be back to judge the finished products."

Lucy and I exchanged glances. If it wasn't any of the competitors, that left only Polly and Noah.

Polly was America's sweetheart. And if it was Noah . . .

maybe he killed Polly. Maybe she got too close to the truth. The thought sent a shiver down my spine.

Lucy fiddled her fingers. I knew she was itching to find out what was going on. She'd expose everything and everyone, and she'd get into Sunderland. Even if I lost and ended up at Fable Creek High (assuming I somehow didn't take the blame for Chef Remi's condition), she'd come here where she belonged.

Instead of terror flitting through my gut, imagining my life without Lucy around me every minute, I focused on how good solving this awful crime would be for her journalism career. She was going to make the world a better place by catching a criminal and always doing the hard thing to get the right answer. I couldn't be selfish. Lucy deserved this. And I knew now that even if we were apart, Lucy wasn't abandoning me. I could stand on my own too.

"You all are so quiet, it's like a cemetery in here!" Noah's laugh lacked humor. "I'm sure you're all nervous. This is it! The final challenge! And it's going to prove to each and every one of you if you have what it takes. Are you ready?"

We all nodded, yet I knew we were thinking very different things. What was Micah about to say? Where was Polly, really? What would happen when the police found out Remi actually was attacked and nearly everyone had a motive?

Chef Noah continued as if we were thrilled and not

silently panicking. "Your last challenge will be to make a holiday showpiece. We want five—yes, five—different cookies. We want them combined into one structure that represents your holiday. You have three hours to wow me and Polly. Think you can do it?"

Philippa and Maeve began chittering among themselves. Jaden nibbled his lip, and Micah looked directly at me, while Lucy was clearly in her own head, plotting. And I realized there were two very serious things happening, and I had to choose which one I wanted to put all my energy into: winning this competition or uncovering a murderer before I and all my new friends were put under a microscope and arrested for something none of us did.

Noah turned to me. "What holiday will you do, Laila?"

I grinned, though I wasn't filled with holiday spirit. "Juneteenth."

"Oh, good choice. I don't know much about the food served for that holiday, which is exciting. Maeve?" Noah looked over at her.

"Eid al-Fitr," she responded slowly.

Then the others answered too. Micah said Chuseok, Philippa said Valentine's Day, and Jaden said Halloween, which Noah seemed particularly excited about—probably because he didn't know or care about the other ones.

"All right, let's get baking, huh?" He sounded like he'd

been a host of his own baking show for years and it was all a polished act.

Once we stepped into the kitchen arena, put on our aprons, and collected our ingredients, it was clear all us competitors hadn't forgotten our conversation in the cafeteria. If we didn't figure out what was going on before the end of this competition, we could all be in very big trouble.

19

Lucy

I'D PLANNED TO fake a headache and skip out on the last round to find the security room, but one look at Noah's smile had made me rethink it. As he'd stood in the doorway of the cafeteria, penning all of us kids in, my stomach flipped. And not just because of those awful-looking sandwiches. Although Laila had made a good point about questioning where all this competition food was coming from, it was clear that most of it was made on day one and expected to last all weekend. Which explained the stale bread and the soggy vegetables. Gross.

But Laila's point about the pizza? There was definitely something fishy about who or what had been leaving the Sunderland grounds, and *how*. I'd originally assumed it was Noah because he'd picked up Chef Remi's medication from the pharmacy that morning, but then how was the pizza still warm at noon, after round one? Pizza delivery folks were heroes, but I doubted they'd brave epic storms and ford streams for a measly tip. If any of that about the storm and roads was true at all.

The uneasiness from this thought, along with the fact that I was second-guessing everything the chefs had said to us all weekend, made me lose my appetite.

Unfortunately, my ability to investigate anything was limited due to the fact that I was now stuck in the kitchen arena with everyone.

Chef Noah paced around the kitchen arena, taking his judging duties super-seriously. Where was Chef Polly? Was she really not feeling well, or was she searching for the security room like she and Noah talked about?

I had to get to that security room first.

I peered around me for any excuse to leave the kitchen arena. Falling off the stool and pretending to hurt myself? No, Laila might stop what she was doing and try to help me. Spilling my water bottle and needing to change clothes? No, that wouldn't buy me enough time. Then I remembered Laila's disgusting, ultra-embarrassing suggestion from yesterday.

Ariella Wilborn would put her ego aside and do what it took to get the story, and that's what I had to do too.

I scrunched up my face, clutched my stomach, and groaned dramatically. "Blaarggghh."

Chef Noah paused his pacing and stared at me. "Please, Lucy, don't distract the competitors."

As he said my name, Laila peered up from her mixing bowl at me. I did the quickest of nods in her direction to let her know I was okay, and her eyes widened with recognition.

I groaned again. "But Chef Noah, I don't feel so good."

He took a step toward me before thinking twice about getting near someone ill. "This is the last round. Can you have some water and wait it out?"

I shook my head and blew out a breath, ready to sacrifice myself for a greater cause. "No, I need to get out of here. I have"—I made an exaggerated, pained face—"diarrhea."

As expected, the other competitors broke out in a chorus of "Yuck!" and "Eww . . ." Laila joined in a second later, but I could tell she was trying desperately to hide her laughter.

Chef Noah put his hands out in front of him, as if that would shield him from catching my fake stomach bug. "Lucy, I'm going to have to ask you to exit the kitchen arena. We can't have you contaminating the competitors' work. Return to your room at once, and stay there. I'll come check on you after we're done."

Excellent. As fast as I could, I gathered my things and dashed toward the door.

As I exited, Jaden's voice followed me.

"Whew, Lucy must really need to go."

I couldn't believe Laila was friends with that kid.

Chef Polly was nowhere to be seen on my way to the security room. I didn't know how much time I had, so I pumped my legs faster.

When I got to the security room door, I slid off my backpack and fished out one of Laila's heavy-duty bobby pins. I picked off the plastic at the end with my nail, then bent the metal like she showed me last night. Holding my breath, I inserted the bobby pin into the lock and got to work. Laila had me practice on our bathroom door a dozen times, but this door lock seemed harder to pick. Or maybe it was the fact that my hands were sweaty and slipping off the pin or that it was so dark down here that I had to squint at what the wire was doing.

After a few minutes of trying, I still had no luck. I wiped my hands off on my pants and tried again. I could practically hear Laila's voice in my ear, urging me to keep going. She had never been one to let me quit when I thought I couldn't do something. Like when I wanted to ditch the middle school paper altogether after I upset that jerk editor in chief Peter and was nervous about being around him. Laila knew what it meant to me to succeed, and she pushed me to stick to it, even if some days were tough.

And maybe that was just the distraction I needed, because when I wiggled the bobby pin this time, I heard a click. I repeated the motion, and seconds later, I turned the doorknob freely. I did it. I unlocked the security room. I leaped up and almost cheered aloud for myself, until I remembered I was supposed to be stealthy and unnoticed.

The security room was small and dark, with the one wall taken up by monitors showing different parts of the school. I exhaled a sigh of relief. At least these security cameras were on, even if the live streaming ones in the kitchen arena weren't. That meant we'd be able to figure out who was moving around the campus and when, and maybe that would show us which of the chefs had an opportunity to hurt Chef Remi.

I could barely see a foot in front of me. I closed the door behind me so I could turn on the lights. The fluorescent bulb overhead flicked on, and it gave off a creepy haunted-house-style buzzing sound. I couldn't wait to find what I needed and get out of this room and the whole eerie basement level fast.

I spotted a keyboard and mouse on the desk underneath the monitors. With a few clacks of the keys, I accessed the security software. It would've been nice if I could brag that I hacked the system thanks to some special Ariella Wilborn–style analytic skills. But nope: folks simply shouldn't keep passwords on a neon-yellow Post-it Note in plain sight.

I settled into the squeaky, high-backed computer chair and pulled up the records from the morning of day one, before the competitors showed up. A black sedan parked in front of the school around eight a.m., and Noah stepped out of the driver's seat. Then he scurried around the car to open the passenger door, and out came Chef Remi, complete with dark, face-shielding glasses. The audio was obscured thanks to the rustling of the leaves from the storm blowing in, but I could tell that Chef Remi didn't utter a "thank you" as Noah carried his bags and bumped Remi's door closed for him. I'd get grounded if I didn't throw out "please" and "thank you" like a flower girl at a wedding.

As Remi turned toward the Sunderland entrance, another black sedan pulled up. This time, a driver in a crisp white shirt held out a hand for Chef Polly to safely place her kitten heels on the curb.

You'd think that folks that work in the same culinary circles for decades longer than I've been alive would at least be civil to each other. Even Jaden, who accused me of murder at some point, acknowledged me when we were in the same room.

But Remi actually spit on the ground when Polly waved

at him. Granted, it wasn't a smooth, beauty pageant–style wave: more of dismissive shooing motion accompanied by pursed lips. It was obvious their dislike was mutual.

"Let me be clear: I'm only here for the children," Polly said to Remi, just barely audible through the leaf shaking. "So you don't exist to me outside the kitchen arena, got it?" Her voice was clipped and meaner than I'd ever imagine from America's sweetheart.

"And let *me* be clear," Remi said, his face emotionless. "I'm only here because this one"—he jutted a thumb back at Noah—"forced me into it. You don't exist to me either."

Then he walked away, leaving Noah bumbling behind him with all their bags, trying to catch up, and Polly standing on the curb with her fists clenched.

I slumped down in my chair, and the plastic and metal underneath me squeaked again. I could've sworn they weren't as mean to each other during the competition, but that could've all been an act. What else wasn't what it seemed? I'd been gone from the kitchen arena for more than ten minutes, and all I'd found was that, yes, Chef Remi was as rude as everyone said he was. If I didn't speed up this process, I could be here all afternoon. It might raise suspicions if I wasn't in my room when Noah swung by to check on me.

Then the click of kitten heels against linoleum made me jump. Chef Polly?

I realized I had the light on, making this the only lit-up room on the whole floor. If that ~~wasn't a Las~~ Vegas–style neon sign pointing "Hello, someone's in here," I didn't know what was. I lunged for the light switch, to buy myself some time.

Instead, the creaky computer chair betrayed me. It let out a long *eeek,* metal against metal, when I rose. The tinny sound rang so loud in my ears that it might as well have been a cannon.

Footsteps stumbled to a stop outside the door. In the sliver of space beneath the door, the dim hallway light was interrupted by an unwelcome shadow. "Who's there?"

I clapped a hand over my mouth. I didn't even want to breathe and give myself away.

Chef Polly tried again. "Show yourself. Now."

A pause. I didn't think my heart beat at that moment.

But it nearly leapt out of my chest when the door handle jiggled. Thankfully, though I'd made rookie mistakes of turning on the light and fumbling with the furniture, I had locked the door. Or, to be honest, I'd forgotten to disable the auto-locking mechanism altogether. I'd been so focused on my goal of combing the camera footage that I'd overlooked this one detail. I counted it as a win anyway.

"Humph. Well, I'm definitely in the right place," Chef Polly muttered to herself. "I'll need to get those school keys from Noah."

Noah had keys? Could he have already deleted evidence?

The second I heard Chef Polly's steps fade, I threw myself back at the computer and clicked recklessly through the next hour or so of footage, hoping for something, anything. It would take no more than five minutes for Chef Polly to get to the kitchen arena and back. And if I wasn't out of here by then . . .

According to the footage, supply trucks drove in and left around nine a.m. I counted the number of people entering, and it was the same number leaving. So none of them stuck around to terrorize a middle school cookie competition. Around the same time, Chef Polly exited the school and rummaged around in her trunk. A murder weapon, maybe? I scooted to the edge of my seat as she tugged out a black leather bag. She reached inside and pulled out a— Wait, was that a wig? That wasn't helpful to our investigation at all. Chef Remi definitely didn't die a death by fabulousness.

But two clicks later, the main entrance of the school swung open again. This time, Chef Remi sauntered out, a newspaper tucked under his arm. Noah stormed out right after him. His face was red, and he waved his arms like he was saying something important. To which Remi made a show of unfolding the newspaper and reading it instead of responding to Noah.

Alarms blared in my mind. It looked like they were having

an argument. Or at least Noah was trying to have one. Chef Remi was ignoring him completely, like reading his horoscope was more important than hearing what his longtime assistant had to say. I turned up the volume on the computer to see if I could make out what Noah was saying, but it was only wind and foliage.

Then, behind all of that, there was a sudden screech: "It's you! Hurry up and help me, then."

I pushed back from the computer. That noise didn't come from the computer speakers at all. That was Chef Polly, and from the volume of it, she was right outside the door.

"Polly, I've had enough of you and all these other snobby chefs telling me what to do."

The casualness in Noah's voice sent chills down my spine. Something was wrong here. I could feel it in my bones, the same way Laila knew precisely the timing between golden brown and burned. I needed to hide until I could figure out what was going on, but there wasn't much furniture in here other than the squeaky chair and the mounted electronics. And what were the chances the two chefs would overlook a kid-shaped heap of clothing a second time?

"Oh, cut out this 'snobby' malarkey," Chef Polly said. "We're not enemies here."

"You seem to think we're not equals either. You really

should have listened to me when I told you to wait until after the round ends."

"Listen to you? You're only here as the backup judge."

Noah snickered, and it suddenly struck me as a dark, sinister thing, like a clown in a PG-13 horror movie. I'd never heard him sound like that.

"You couldn't be further from the truth, Polly. You're all here *because* of me. If you'd simply done as I asked, we could've come to the security room together, after we'd announced the Golden Cookie winner and the children were busy packing up their bags. That would've given me enough time to figure out which brat tipped off the police, then erase the full three days' worth of footage—by accident, of course, as incompetent, emotionally fragile assistants do. But no, you had to interrupt me in the middle of the round because you wanted to start reviewing the footage by yourself. And I can't trust you to do that."

I couldn't help the gasp that escaped me. Thankfully—or not—Chef Polly's own gasp overwhelmed the sound I'd made. We were here because of Noah? Suddenly, puzzle pieces began to line up in my mind: all those suspicions we had about why the other competitors were here, the odd details about the storm and the roads, how we'd been relying on the big binder of rules that Noah had handed us on day one. Somehow, Noah orchestrated this whole weekend in a way that would have made Chef Remi's death seem natural and, even if it looked fishy, made every other person here a valid suspect. And now he was trying to cover his tracks.

I fumbled for my phone. Not like I'd be able to reach anyone from the basement, but at least I could record what Noah was doing.

"You know what? You're not the one listening, honey," Chef Polly said. These adults sounded way too businesslike given the fact that they were talking about deleting critical evidence in an attempted murder case. "When I said you and I weren't enemies, that's the truth. I think we want the same thing, for none of this . . . messiness to get out into the world."

Her words made me pause.

"All I want right now is that security footage gone, and I need to be the one to do it. So if you don't move, Polly, I'm going to make you." I barely had time to sort through what Polly said because all I could hear then was the jingle of metal against metal: keys. This room, already too small, suddenly felt the size of a shoebox, and I was some poor insect that got trapped inside by a bully. I didn't have a second to figure out if there was anything I could use to defend myself. If only I'd brought that wooden spoon!

There was a click, like I heard earlier when I used Laila's

bobby pins. My heart thunked into my stomach. My grip around my phone tightened.

The door opened, and I was face-to-face with the people who may have tried to kill Chef Remi.

And from the way their faces went from shock to rage when they saw me, I might not make it out of here alive.

20

Laila

THE KITCHEN WAS a mess of movement and dirty pans and burned cookies. No one was focused. No one was competing right now. Lucy had been gone maybe twenty minutes, and during that time, I hadn't started a single baked item.

Five minutes ago, Chef Noah left us to go talk to Chef Polly, who appeared in the doorway for only a second before waving him over to her. She didn't look particularly sick to me, but then again, I could barely see her through the bright lights beaming down on us. With a smile, Chef Noah said he'd be back, yet the way he spoke made us all stop and shiver. He didn't sound like himself. He sounded like . . . well, like he was going to do something bad. He looked grim, determined. Angry.

The moment he left, we all crumbled. Philippa held

Maeve, who was sobbing uncontrollably. Micah banged a pound of butter way too hard with a rolling pin, while Jaden set his sheet pan down on the table and let out a long sigh.

"It could only be Noah or Polly." Jaden looked over at me as if my opinion was the only one he needed. "I don't understand why. Or how."

Micah dropped the rolling pin. "The morning we—me, Laila, and Philippa—arrived, we set our bags down in our rooms super fast and then we came here." He gestured to the kitchen arena. "We only had a moment in our rooms, but I threw my stuff in, and I was about to leave when . . . I saw Noah come into the room behind me real quick and put something in his pocket. I thought he was coming to hurry me up. He acted like everything was normal. Later, after Chef Remi . . . you know, and we got curfewed into our rooms, I started to think it wasn't normal."

Jaden stared at him, his face twisting. "And you didn't think to mention any of this earlier?"

Micah rolled his eyes. "Uh, I tried. I was sorta overwhelmed with Chef Remi almost dying! And the adults kept saying his collapse was natural or it was Laila—sorry, Laila—and I can't imagine what Noah was doing in our room. . . ."

"Your medicine," I hissed suddenly, surprising myself. "What if Noah took one of the pills and gave Remi your medicine instead of his heart stuff? What if—"

"Um, guys?" Philippa and Maeve clutched each other closer as the lights began to flicker in the room. "Do you think it's the storm or . . . ?"

I watched the lights go off and on almost methodically. There was only one thought in my head. Lucy. It had to be Lucy. And that meant Noah must've tried to kill Remi, he might've killed Polly, and now he was going to kill Lucy. She'd found the security room. She was messing with the circuit breakers so it made the building's lights flicker, the way she signaled me at her little brother's party that one time, to let me know she was in big deadly trouble. Oh no.

"What is it, Laila?" Maeve looked at me with such concern that I wished I could answer her. Instead my heart was pounding in my ears and threatening to burst from my chest. My body was shaking and begging to get out of here.

I opened my mouth, but no words came out. Nothing at all. The lights suddenly stopped flickering, and I knew it was time to do something.

"Maeve, keep calling the police until you get through. Noah's up to no good," Micah said, as if reading my mind.

"Lucy," I finally managed, my mouth dry.

"We have to save her." As if he were Thor, Jaden picked up a rubber mallet we used in chocolate preparation.

Philippa removed her engraved round knife from its

sheath and Micah grabbed his rolling pin. I seized a whisk—it might not be helpful at all, but it made me feel a little safer. Despite us wielding our tools, I could tell none of us wanted to use them.

Maeve darted out of the room toward the phones. Philippa, Micah, Jaden, and I scrambled in the other direction, holding our kitchen tools, toward the part of the building we hadn't spent any time in. This side of the hallway was definitely shinier, as if it hadn't seen too much action since school let out a few weeks ago. It smelled clean, like lemon soap. Everything was so pretty and polished, and . . . the same. How was I supposed to find Lucy?

"Where would they go?" Philippa asked.

"The security room." The words streamed from my mouth as if a few seconds ago I hadn't nearly lost the ability to speak. "Lucy was going to investigate. She's . . ." My voice trailed off. She never told me where the room was, never told me anything about the layout of this school. Panic fluttered in my gut. This school was big, and my friend was somewhere inside it without me. She had to be terrified. She had to be in danger.

Micah's hands plopped on my shoulders. "We're going to find her." He was so mighty. Mighty cool and brave, and I thought he might like me, but most of all I was really lucky he became my friend. He and Philippa, Maeve, and Jaden.

But right then, the most important person in my life besides Mom needed me, needed us. He seemed to notice that and pulled away.

"Security room? I think I know where that is," Jaden said as he sidled up next to me. "Charlie once told me that he and his friends sometimes hang in an old rec room in the basement, and they have to be quiet because the guards are next door. That must be the security room. Come on."

We followed after him quickly, clutching our tools like beloved stuffed animals that'd save us from the monsters under our beds. Or in this case, the monster that had my best friend and might be a murderer.

I couldn't understand why Noah would do this. But I wasn't Lucy—I couldn't focus on a million details and somehow come to the right conclusion. All I could do was bake and be her friend; she was the brilliant one. She was the one who figured out the bad guy in every mystery movie we watched, the one who walked these unknown halls in search of the truth. And now she had found it . . . and it could get her killed.

We rushed down the stone steps to the basement before Philippa threw her arms out, telling us to stop. From down the hall came yells, cries. There were two doors on either side at the end. On the right, there was the rec room. On the left, there was security, as Jaden thought. I gulped, and we snuck forward a few inches to investigate the noise.

"Let us out! You'll never get away with this!" Chef Polly screeched. "Do you have any idea who I am? People know I'm here. There's no—" And then her voice cut off with an *oof.*

"We have to—" I began to whisper before Philippa shushed me. Right. We had to keep the element of surprise.

Micah gripped his rolling pin tighter as Jaden crept ahead. When his hand drifted toward the doorknob, a defiant voice rang through the thick door.

"Polly's right: you won't get away with this. If I found out, I bet you the others did too. Laila won't stop till you're behind bars." Lucy sounded like she was standing tall, hands on her hips, strong as a steel bull. Hearing her sent pangs of panic spiraling around my stomach. I prepared to use my whisk like I was going to whack Noah.

Because I was going to whack him. Hard.

No one threatened my best friend.

I shouldered past the others and reached for the doorknob . . . only it didn't budge. My eyes almost bulged out of their sockets. I pounded on the metal door instead. "Lucy!"

"Laila!" she screamed. "It's Noah, he's—"

But then she went quiet and left me terrified about what was happening on the other side of the door. Did he hurt her? Cover her mouth? What had he done to Lucy?

"Lucy!"

There was only silence.

"Lucy!" I screamed again. I was about to throw myself against the door when it cracked open and Noah stepped out, shutting it carefully behind him. I staggered back, and we all stood there, gobsmacked as to what to say or do. Well, not me. "Where's Lucy?"

"Lucy is fine," Noah said with a big smile that didn't reach his eyes. "*If* you children do as I say." He clapped his hands together, drawing our attention. He hovered over us in his villainous glory. "Go upstairs and finish baking, then go home and don't say a word about what you've witnessed. Because the way I see it, all of you have a motive, and no one can prove a thing. The truth is, any of us could have hurt Remi. I don't . . . I didn't . . ." His voice trailed off as he lost a bit of his steam.

Noah was right, and from the way Philippa, Micah, and Jaden froze, they knew it. There was a reason they were all picked. Noah had done it all.

"You—" Noah pointed to Philippa and Micah. "Remi nearly bankrupted both of your families. You came here looking for revenge."

"That was so long ago." Micah's eyes narrowed. "We believe in our food and our restaurant. Remi tried, but he couldn't touch us."

"I'm sure that's what your parents told you to get you to sleep at night. Mommy and Daddy didn't want to share that big, bad Remi was planning on opening a Korean barbecue joint using his star power to put little Fable Falls on the map next month, did they?" Noah sneered and turned to Jaden. "Your daddies almost got booted out of the filmmaking world after Remi smeared their names everywhere in the business. Without him, they can rebuild their reputations. And surprise, surprise, you knew the layout of the school, you got here before everyone else. You could have deleted the footage, turned the cameras off. All the fingers will point at you. You have the bad attitude, quick to blame anyone and everyone else. You, who brought unpermitted drugs to campus."

Jaden lowered his rubber mallet, mouth open. He was going to be the fall guy all along—at least before I showed up unannounced. That was why Noah talked a biased Remi into letting him compete. He knew about Jaden's medicine, about his fathers' troubles, about how his sour attitude would alienate the rest of us so we wouldn't defend him. With how well Noah put all these pieces together, the police were going to look right past Noah and throw Jaden in handcuffs instead.

We needed proof. *I* needed Lucy.

"And me?" I asked, my lips curling as my fingers clung to

my metal whisk, which threatened to melt in the heat of my palm. "What possible motive could I have?"

"You weren't supposed to be here, but if I had to spin a tale it would be easy. You are the poorest, the most desperate, and though you may have won the first round, Remi still had some harsh words for you. You couldn't let him tank your only chance of attending this prestigious school." Noah looked away as if I didn't matter, like I was a fruit fly in a room of spiders. "Where's Maeve? She's got a motive too. Don't be fooled by her sweetness—"

"You leave Maeve alone," Philippa said, her lips wobbling. She was not the Philippa who made people tremble in her presence. She was scared too. Noah had them all figured out. He had them cornered.

"Why did you do this?" I stepped closer to him, peering into his eyes until he looked away awkwardly.

Noah's hand twitched by his side. "Eleven years I worked for him. Eleven years I sacrificed and he never said thank you, wouldn't give me the career he kept promising. Every opportunity, every promotion I pleaded for, he said no. And this last time . . . this last time he threatened to expose everything I did. Everything I did for him! I lied, begged, and stole *for* him. He would've been nowhere without me, and that's why he was never going to let me go, never going to make me a star. I knew too much and I was too good of an assistant."

A few of the competitors gasped when his words sank in: Noah not only might know the reasons their families ran into trouble with Chef Remi, but he also might've been behind it all. Noah might've been as bad as—or worse than—the chef everyone hated.

Noah shook his head. "Chef Remi loved a good cheat and hated doing the reputable thing. . . . It was my job to find him a failing restaurant, throw his name on it, make easy money, and sell it before people could wise up to the quick flip. It should have been no surprise that he cheated me for as long as he did when that was how he made his millions." He huffed, the anger building in his voice. "I wanted revenge. I deserved it. Then one day I was managing his schedule and saw this rinky-dink children's cookie competition invitation to judge and took it, knowing I could isolate him out here at Sunderland. I could finally take him down. Make him pay."

Philippa inhaled sharply, and I could tell she was thinking of her own family and how Chef Remi almost ruined them.

"You planned every detail from the 'flooded roads' to the choice of competitors and the sandwiches you prepped on the first day with the acidic pesto when you built yourself an alibi," I said, just the way Lucy would have if she weren't locked in a room. "'Poor Noah' was run ragged by the competition. Every absence could be explained away by making our food, cleaning our messes, helping Polly." Lucy would tell me to keep him talking, and that's what I did. The more he talked, the more time we had till the police came.

Noah's glower deepened as he nodded. "I set up the qualification rounds. Helped the selection committee. Sunderland was only too happy for my assistance. All of you were my clueless pawns, and I moved you on my chessboard. Jaden even took the kind of pills that would react poorly with Chef Remi's heart medicine but make the rest of us only feel a tad fluttery. Everything I've ever wanted was within my grasp." He clenched his fists as if revenge were a real, squeezable thing. "Then Chef Remi did what he does best—ruin dreams. Especially mine, like I was a fly in his soup." He sighed then, more frustrated than ashamed. "The thing is, I wanted to kill him. The plan was in motion, and then . . . and then I couldn't do it. I didn't swap the medicine."

"Yeah, right. How come my medicine is all gone?" Jaden cut in.

Noah rolled his eyes. "I only took one pill, kid. I stole the bottle and left it in the walk-in right after I got everyone to round one the first day."

"You're lying. Saying anything to cover your tracks. The medicine is crumbled up all over the cookies. Not Jaden's tea mixture, the actual heavy-duty medicine." I held my whisk out threateningly. "Nice try."

"I didn't—I didn't hurt him. Did I?" He shook his head, unsure of himself. "Anyway, it still worked out, right? His heart did the dirty work for me. But if they see the footage . . . they'll think . . ." He shook his head again. "I need to get out of here, fast and far, until this mess dies down. So a bunch of children won't stand in my way if they know what's good for them, will they?" He made eye contact with each of us, intimidating and scary. Menacing.

None of us answered, instead stewing in our anger and worry. This guy was next-level evil, planning to take down everyone and everything for revenge. If he didn't have Lucy, I would stand in his face and tell him that I would scream out the truth to everyone in the world until he paid for what he'd done. But I took a step back in defeat, and so did Micah. And Jaden. We'd lost.

Until the door smashed open and Lucy stood there. Head held high, torn plastic tape on her wrist, one hand behind her back. When Noah whirled around, Lucy's voice took on a fiery edge I'd never heard from her before. "You forgot to take my pen. . . ." And then she swung her other arm around. "And my phone. I got everything, confession and all."

I beamed at her.

Noah wobbled back. "No one will believe you, any of you. Delete it, Lucy, and I'll let you and Laila walk out of here without suspicion."

"Too late, darling," Chef Polly called from inside the room. "I found the jammed Wi-Fi and turned it on. I may be old and you may think you had me cowed for a moment there, but you lost. Now Lucy, honey, who did you send it to?"

Lucy smiled like a cat that caught a mouse. I couldn't have been more proud of her. This was the Lucy I'd known was in there, who I tried to coax out when that jerk editor in chief Peter kept trying to stamp out her journalistic brilliance. I wanted to see more of this Lucy from now on. She was a force to be reckoned with, just like Dad used to call me. "I sent it to Ariella Wilborn. And *Fable Creek Daily News*. And Mom and Dad. I sent it everywhere."

"Honey, your goose is cooked," Polly said as she limped into the doorway, bracing on the frame for support. Her smile was wild and almost wicked.

"No," I corrected. "Your cookie's crumbled."

Philippa whooped, Micah laughed, and Jaden grinned at me. Which distracted me from Noah, who lunged in my direction. I stood between him and the stairway to escape.

My muscles tensed for impact, but Micah threw himself

between us and smacked Noah right in the chest with the rolling pin.

Noah let out a whoosh of air and doubled over. Jaden snuck up behind him and smashed him with the rubber mallet, which made Noah throw up his hands and shove the boys down.

I gripped my whisk tight. He still had to get through me.

Noah only scowled as Jaden and Micah slowly picked themselves back up. A tired-looking Polly, her wig askew, leaned on Lucy, and Philippa brandished her knife, though at any second it'd tumble out of her hand since she was shaking so hard.

"You hurt Chef Remi. You locked up Chef Polly. And you threatened my best friend. This is for them," I said, wielding my whisk like a sword.

Noah's big, droopy eyes found mine as he clutched his center. "I told you I didn't do it! I—"

"We know it was you." Polly's voice took on a harsh, shrill note, and she stood straighter than a moment ago.

"But the pill, I swear I tossed it—"

"No one will believe you. Everything happened the way you planned it. Soon everyone will know. You're a coward, and cowards always lose." Polly's voice cracked on "coward" and she suddenly looked so small and so . . . angry. None of us had anything to say to that. We knew Polly was mad—but this was next-level. Lucy and I exchanged a glance.

And in that moment I was looking at her, Noah ran at me again. I wasn't sure if he was attacking me or trying to flee, but I still swung at him with everything I had.

21

Lucy

NOAH DIDN'T STAND a chance. Laila knocked the breath out of him with one strong, strategic swing.

If he'd asked me—which he wouldn't have, because he was a scheming criminal—taking on a bunch of kids who spent all day kneading and hand-mixing things and were armed? Not the best idea. Kitchen tools were as good as throwing stars and batons in their skilled hands. They could do some damage.

And damage Laila did.

Noah staggered back and tripped over Maeve's outstretched foot. Silent as a spy, Maeve had crept down to the basement after calling the police on the landline, to deliver this crushing blow.

As he fell, Noah bumped his head on the wall behind

him and let out a stunned groan. He slumped down on the ground.

He was right about one thing: do not underestimate Maeve.

"Polly, the tape!" I yelled.

Polly tossed me the plastic tape roll. With Philippa slicing up long strips with her knife, we quickly bound Noah's hands and feet, the way he did to Polly and me earlier. Polly even added a little bow around Noah's feet. Presentation really did matter.

Laila wrapped me in a hug then, half yelling and half sniffling about how worried she'd been about me.

"You did it," I said as her sniffles tapered off. "You caught the wannabe murderer!"

Laila pulled back from our hug, smiling. "Technically, I only knocked him out. You tied him up. *We* caught the wannabe murderer!"

It was my turn to wrap her in a hug. I came to the Golden Cookie Competition simply hoping to build out my writing samples for the Ariella Wilborn Journalism Scholarship: a sumptuous foodie piece and a soulful profile on my best friend. Though an attempted murder was nowhere near what any of us (besides Noah) wanted, this was my chance to write something not only meaningful but explosive. I had all I needed to write a piece that would show everyone, including that jerk editor in chief Peter, that I had what it takes. And if I needed more details, I wasn't going to let anyone's hurt feelings—not even my own—stop me from getting the truth.

But it didn't escape my notice that Laila didn't get what she wanted. In fact, she'd ditched the last round early to come save me, choosing me over her dream. Now I had to find a way to make everyone see Laila had what it takes too.

"Kids, are you all right?" a voice bellowed down the hallway at us.

We all whirled around, the competitors wielding their tools like light sabers.

A tall Black woman with gold-rimmed glasses and sparkly brown eyes jogged toward us. She was in a Sunderland Academy hoodie and yoga pants, like someone pulled her straight out of brunch to come here for this disaster. It was Principal Winters.

That meant someone was able to reach us on campus. The roads were clear. We could go home. I was so relieved I could cry.

All of us, even Chef Polly, seemed to have the same idea: make a good impression on the principal. The competitors corrected their postures and hid their kitchen tools behind their backs. Chef Polly adjusted her wig.

The principal paused in front of us and her eyes swept

around, assessing the situation. "I came as soon as the police alerted us about the tip. I'm so glad to see you kids safe."

Her gaze dipped to Noah, trussed in duct tape, and her lips pursed. "Noah? What's going on here? You're supposed to be the competition coordinator, the face of Sunderland to these young folks."

Noah, beginning to awaken, grunted in response. He couldn't answer through the tape across his mouth.

"Oh, he coordinated, all right," I said. "He set up the Golden Cookie Competition so perfectly that he was prepared to blame everyone here for Chef Remi getting hurt or killed."

Principal Winters's jaw dropped. "Noah? Really? It's a good thing the police are on their way. They'll get to the bottom of this."

Polly politely coughed and stepped forward. "Principal Winters, if I may." She smoothed back the stray hairs on her wig and tugged down her crumpled blouse. She was back to being TV-ready America's sweetheart. "There's no need to dig further. Noah St. John single-handedly tried to kill Chef Remi, and the children can prove it."

I nodded. "I have notes, recordings. I think the police should probably investigate too, right?"

Chef Polly's TV smile curved into a sneer when she looked at me. "Lucy, honey, I thought you were a smart girl, with a promising journalism future. But if you're not con-fident about this, you're always going to be a failure. Like Noah here."

For a second, my heart squeezed like she'd reached into my chest and grabbed it. Days ago, I would've lowered my head and slunk away, tossed my notebook in the trash. But the work Laila and I did this weekend was real, serious, and exactly the kind of investigative journalism I knew I was capable of. Thanks to us, a bad guy was tied up for trying to kill Chef Remi. That should have been the end of our big, victorious story.

So why was Chef Polly acting strangely?

"Polly, that's a little harsh, isn't it?" Principal Winters said carefully.

Polly snorted, a crude sound wholly unlike anything she made on her last TV show. "You weren't stuck with these—um, lively children for the whole weekend." She brushed her hand against her forehead then, disturbing the wig again. It was like she was unable to set it straight on her head and it was bugging the heck out of her.

She sighed dramatically. "You know, I do believe I'm feeling faint. If y'all will excuse me, I'm going to go lie down. This has all been so overwhelming."

Principal Winters moved aside, but not before Laila and I made eye contact. She felt it too. Something was off. And this was no time to be timid.

Laila took a step to the side, placing herself between Chef Polly and the exit. "Not before you apologize to my friend."

"It's all right, Laila. I don't need an apology." I raised my chin and looked Chef Polly straight in the eye. "I am confident. I researched the suspects, discovered the cameras were off, and learned to pick a lock. More importantly, I learned to follow my gut and tell the story, even if it meant ruffling some feathers. And from the looks of it, your feathers are a mess, Chef Polly. There's something you're not telling us."

The chef's gaze flared like someone had turned up the dial on the stove. "How dare you. Noah's the one you want. He even confessed to switching out the medicine!"

"But then he backed out," I said. The puzzle pieces that had clicked together so well earlier suddenly rearranged. "You hated Chef Remi as much as Noah did."

Philippa and Maeve moved to stand on either side of Laila.

"That's right," Philippa said. "You were so quick to pin everything on him. But you're one of the judges. You had some responsibility during the competition, didn't you?"

Maeve planted her hands on her hips. "And we know about your TV show. It was on all the gossip blogs."

"What?" Laila and I said together.

Maeve blinked. "I thought everyone knew. Chef Polly

was being replaced with Chef Remi, on her own show! Well, she *was*."

Polly's hands clenched into fists. "Move out of the way, young ladies. You have no clue what you're talking about."

Now Jaden and Micah angled to block the chef's way too.

"Mmpp," Noah grunted from the floor.

"I said, move!" Chef Polly screeched then.

Even Principal Winters flinched at the sound, but everyone stayed planted. Laila nodded at me. No way she was letting Polly pass.

Polly stomped a foot, like a toddler having a tantrum, and her wig slid down another centimeter.

"Your wig," I whispered. "Something's keeping it from resting properly."

All it took was Polly's eyes widening to know that I had stumbled upon something.

"You can't prove anything!" she shrieked. Her hands shot up to secure her wig like it was a hat about to sail off in the wind. At the same time, Noah lurched forward and slammed against her hip, sending her hands flailing and the wig flying down the hall.

A small baggie slipped off from its place on Polly's head and landed on Noah's shoulder. I reached it first. Polly started to sputter an excuse, but I ignored her as I inspected the baggie's contents. A memory from the first day—orange bottles and spilled water—crashed into me.

"Are . . . are these Chef Remi's pills?" I said.

At that, Noah nodded his head roughly and gurgled something that sounded like a yes.

I handed the baggie to Principal Winters. "These should probably go to the police, as evidence."

"I agree. They'll need to test everything. And Lucy, that was a good question," Principal Winters said, gripping the baggie tightly. "A question that you, Polly, need to stay right here and answer."

Polly scowled. "You can't prove anything."

Laila bumped her shoulder against mine. "You're underestimating Lucy here. We've got witnesses, notes, and soon we'll have camera footage and lab results."

"And proof that you were up to no good literally just fell out of your wig, lady," Micah piped up.

My best friend's faith in me made me braver. "I saw Chef Remi take his pill, but if you have the real ones, then you must've given him something else. Something worse."

"Chef Remi made a name for himself as having the most well-developed, and therefore pickiest, palate," Laila cut in. "Polly, why would you think you'd get away with switching out his pills with something poisonous without him noticing?"

At this, Chef Polly's cookies seemed to crumble. She

cackled like it was the funniest thing she'd ever heard. "The most well-developed palate? Ha! Remi was an untalented fraud! If your beloved chef's taste buds truly deserved all that acclaim, he would've tasted the difference in the medicine. You said so yourself."

The horror over the fact that the real murderer was right there, in front of me, was quickly overshadowed by shock that my gut was right.

"Noah held on to Chef Remi's medicine. Are you saying Noah was in on it?"

"Mmp," Noah said. Part of me wanted to rip the duct tape off his mouth, but Laila shook her head ever so slightly: we'd all had enough of that guy.

Chef Polly crossed her arms. "See? Noah just confessed to everything again. Didn't you catch that?"

Everyone—including Noah—rolled their eyes at Polly's sad last-ditch effort to get out of this.

"Quit the lying," Philippa said. "Lucy and Laila have you cornered. You can't hide a thing from them. The more you lie, the worse you'll look. If that's even possible."

Anger burned in Polly's eyes. "Well, I had my own plan, but I didn't know Noah was up to something too until I saw him sneaking out of Jaden's room. Then I quickly pieced together what he was trying to do. I'd heard little Jaden took medicine for headaches or what have you, and from my critically acclaimed guest host stint on *The Morning Panel* during American Heart Month, I remembered that medicine that affects blood flow probably wouldn't react too well with heart pills like Remi's. The only smart thing Noah has ever done, if you ask me. I hoped Noah would do the job . . . a pity he didn't have the guts for it after all. But *I* did. He, like all of you, easily believed I was just a bumbling old lady—no one would suspect America's sweetheart."

"If Noah wasn't in on it, how'd you get Jaden's medicine?" I asked.

"I was keeping an eye on Noah, and when I followed him into the walk-in, I saw the pills and knew that he'd backed out. I had the genius idea to use Jaden's pills as a cherry on top of my plan, a way to cover my tracks. I had already swapped Remi's real pills with poison earlier in the day, and I couldn't ditch them with you kids swarming this school like cockroaches. Then as I locked away the cookies as evidence, I sprinkled Jaden's medicine on top of them all. That way, it would look like it could have been *any* of us who hurt Chef Remi and therefore none of us. Too bad it all wasn't enough to kill him. Measuring out black market pills isn't quite the same as measuring out cake flour."

Laila gasped. "And you were going to let Noah take the fall just now? That's messed up."

"Please." Chef Polly crossed her arms. "That little rat

doesn't need your sympathy. You should be on my side! Noah was willing to frame any one of you if he'd gone through with his plan! You should be grateful I intervened. The culinary world is better off without Chef Remi in it. I dare any of you here to swear otherwise."

The silence that followed confirmed how much we all disliked the man. But that didn't mean he should've been nearly killed. I knew where Chef Polly was coming from: it was awful to have your talent overlooked time and time again because there was some mean guy taking all your light, all your opportunities. In my case, it just drove me to try a different tack to get around that jerk editor in chief, not attempt to poison him and cast blame on a bunch of kids. Maybe Chef Polly's puppet cooking show would've been a hit. Now we'd never know.

Because as if they were standing by, waiting for her confession, three police officers appeared at the far end of the hall.

A tall Afro-Latino officer with a grim set to his brow nodded at me, and I caught the hint of respect in his small smile. "Nice work. You may remember me. I'm Detective Valdez. We'll take it from here."

22

Laila

HOURS LATER, WE were all sitting at a few tree-shaded cafeteria tables outside the building we'd spent the last three days in. Detective Valdez asked us to wait outside until our parents arrived—they were going to do some more questioning. There was an officer hanging out at another table to make sure none of us kids tried to run off or something, but it was still nice to get some fresh air for once. The storm clouds were off in the distance, and the sun shone enough to dry everything while not making it all icky and humid.

Cookie dough stuck to my apron, and my hands shook. Sure, from attacking Noah and from . . . everything, but also because they wanted to be back in the kitchen. Fighting for the chance to win a scholarship. That was all over now. I had no regrets; I was only disappointed our hopes were ruined by adults with vendettas.

Jaden and Micah plopped down on both sides of me, while Philippa and Maeve slid onto the bench next to Lucy.

Principal Winters had gathered us here for a final talk while we were waiting. "I got a call from the hospital, and they said Chef Remi has woken up. Once the police lab analyzed Polly's black market pills and figured out what chemicals he had taken, they were able to dull their effects. They expect him to make a full recovery in time."

I didn't ever think I'd smile at the thought of mean Chef Remi being fine, but here we were.

The principal continued. "I wanted to thank you all personally for your heroism this weekend and apologize that it came to this. You were supposed to be competing for the prestigious Golden Cookie award and scholarship, not dealing with attempted murder. . . ."

I looked at Lucy, who was watching the principal with a grimace, and then I lowered my head. I needed that scholarship—we both did. We were talented enough to excel at Sunderland next year, but without that scholarship and admission for me, I wouldn't get the chance.

I raised my hand, awkwardly, because wasn't that what you're supposed to do at school?

Principal Winters smiled. "Yes, Laila?"

"So what now? Are we going to recompete?"

Lucy huffed. "After all we've been through, that doesn't make sense. Sunderland was supposed to be running a safe, fun competition, and they let terrible people like Noah and Polly pull all the strings."

I and the other competitors grumbled in agreement. We were all still shocked to hear how much Noah worked to set up Chef Remi's possible murder, everything down to faking the road closures and cutting all but one landline to keep us from getting too suspicious. He didn't count on having a change of heart or having a more vindictive Chef Polly lurking around. Nor did he factor in having Lucy around to foil both their plans.

Principal Winters nodded thoughtfully. "You're right. That's on us. We should've done our due diligence, and I pledge that we'll do better in the future."

"Psh," Jaden sneered. "What good is the future? What do *we* get, right now?"

Micah stifled a laugh. To be fair, all of us were thinking the same thing.

Even Principal Winters chuckled quietly. She looked at us then, and I could practically see the gears turning in her head. She was standing in front of five of the best bakers in the area and one really incredible journalist. There was one big way she could reward us, and I was about to suggest it when she started speaking.

"How about I make a couple of phone calls and make sure the rest of the Sunderland board agrees with extending admission offers and full scholarships to each of you talented bakers?"

The group broke out into excited chatter before Lucy cut in. "And what about me? I'm not a baker." Her question came out a little shaky: she looked worried.

I had to be there for my best friend. I looked the principal in the eye. "Lucy's a journalist, and she's the one who did all the work unraveling this thing and digging into your easily hackable surveillance system."

Lucy sat up straighter. "I was going to write about the competition. I mean, I still *am* going to write about it, but with all the good and bad parts too."

The principal tipped her head in Lucy's direction, considering, and Lucy didn't back down.

Finally, Principal Winters smiled. "Then it sounds like we owe you our gratitude, Lucy, and we'd be honored if you'd choose to bring your sharp, investigative mind to our school too—with that full scholarship, of course. We'd appreciate it if you keep a few details about the surveillance system under wraps until the police finish their investigation."

Our mouths fell open. Lucy and I were both going to

Sunderland next year and getting it paid for? Not in a million years did I think that this one weekend would result in this. Then again, not in a million years did I think we'd be investigating the almost murder of a prominent chef to clear my own name.

We. Were. Going. To. Sunderland. The two of us. Together.

My heart hammered in my chest. Lucy did this. She did what it took to solve the case, even if it made some of us— even her best friend at one point—angry. She was on her way to becoming the best journalist ever, better than that Ariella lady for sure. And I was going to be there, watching her succeed in all things.

Detective Valdez waved Principal Winters over, and she excused herself to go talk to him. Meanwhile, Jaden, Maeve, Philippa, and Micah swiveled around in their seats so that we were all facing each other. We didn't know a lot about each other when we first arrived—heck, we didn't like each other. Lucy had *dossiers* on these folks pointing out their weaknesses! Still, a sort of friendship had settled easily between us. Maybe we'd be friends in school too. I mean, friends who experienced attempted murder together have to stick together, right?

I cast that thought aside while I untied my apron strings. "Well, if I'm not going to get a fancy Golden Cookie trophy to put on my mom's desk, the least they could give me was this full ride."

We laughed, and Maeve did a quiet snort-giggle thing.

"I wanted to win too," Jaden said. "I guess this means we all get to hang out freshman year."

Philippa and Maeve exchanged warm looks.

"It's perfect," Philippa said.

Maeve's eyes lit up. "And we don't have to wait till next year, we can hang out anytime. Goodness knows there's a ton of Sunderland banquets and dinners we'll be invited to."

"And there's all those new-student and welcome-back events too," Jaden added. "Charlie says they have the best food at these things. No sad sandwiches with pesto."

I couldn't help but smile at him—probably because he'd managed to speak without insulting someone, for once—and Micah cut in with a cough. "If you need help on that article, Lucy, I can convince my parents to let you interview them." He was speaking to her, but he was very clearly looking at me.

Jaden leaned forward. "And with my dads' connections, I can get your articles in the *Times* or somewhere else big. They know Ariella Wilborn!" he said, looking at me too. Weird.

Lucy laughed, her eyes finding mine. I knew what she was thinking. Only I could walk into a cookie competition a ball of nerves and leave with glowing praise from world-renowned chefs, free admission to our dream school, and maybe (?) two kids crushing on me. What could I say? There was nowhere I couldn't go. Nothing I couldn't do, even without Lucy by my side, but especially with Lucy by my side.

"You two really are a great team," Maeve said with a smile. "You should keep up this detective work. Hey, you might make a good amount of cash through it over the summer or during the school year."

I grinned at Lucy. "I love that idea! What do you think, Lucy? I bake 'em, you bust 'em!"

She stared down at the closed notebook between us. With as much as Lucy and I had written—including all those too-long descriptions of Micah's arms—there were plenty of blank pages left. I bet she was imagining what Ariella Wilborn would do.

She clicked her pen. "You bake 'em, I bust 'em."

ACKNOWLEDGMENTS

Creating a perfectly twisty cookie mystery was tough—and delicious—work! We're lucky to have had the very best help. So here goes!

Thank you to:

YOU, the reader. Thank you for picking up this book and taking a chance on our story. We hope you had a fun time reading this and that you found the best cookie accompaniment while you tried to solve our whodunit. Your happiness means the world to us.

Our incredible editor, Jennifer Ung. Your joy and enthusiasm for this project made this story so exciting to work on, and it became the strongest it could be because of you. Thank you; it's been such a pleasure, and we can't wait for the next one!

The entire Quill Tree team! Andrea Vandergrift, Diobelle

Cerna, Mikayla Lawrence, Sona Vogel, Stephanie Evans, Sean Cavanagh, Rosemary Brosnan, Suzanne Murphy, Jean McGinley, Robby Imfeld, Sammy Brown, Patty Rosati, Tara Feehan, Laura Raps, Kerry Moynagh, and the Harper sales team.

Our agents, Natalie Lakosil and Katelyn Detweiler. Thank you for working with and believing in us. Thanks for getting this book out into the world!

To our families, Rahul, Ruby, Raja, Christoph, and Liv. We might've bugged you with our daily research into baking shows and recipe development, but we know you all loved the sweet results. Thanks for being our sounding boards, taste testers, inspirations, support systems, and cheerleaders. We couldn't do this without you.

Lastly, thank you to the librarians, teachers, book bloggers, BookTokkers, bookstagrammers, booksellers, reviewers, and the entire book community—we get to keep writing stories because you tell the world to keep reading them.

Thank you for all that you do.